Mysteries and Misadventures:
Tales from the Highlands

AARON MULLINS

DEDICATION

The Highlands: a beautiful place, with a rich heritage and wonderful people. If you aren't already lucky enough to live there, make sure you visit. This book came from a single promise, made many years ago, now kept.

"There's no place on earth with more of the old superstitions and magic mixed into its daily life than the Scottish Highlands."

- Diana Gabaldon, Outlander

AARON MULLINS

FICTION
Mullins Collection of Best New Fiction
Mullins Collection of Best New Horror
Mysteries and Misadventures: Tales from the Highlands

WRITING GUIDES
How to Write Fiction: A Creative Writing Guide

BUSINESS GUIDES
How to Write a Business Plan
The Ultimate Business Plan Template

PSYCHOLOGY: ACADEMIC
Ethnic Differences in Perceptions of Social Responsibility
Risk Perception in Extreme Event Decision Making
The Effect of Mate Value on Self-esteem
Impact of Social Responsibility on Community Resilience
Enhancing Community Resilience to Flooding
Flood Hazards: Impacts and Responses (chapter)
Social Responsibility and Community Resilience: a
Definition, Context and Methodology
and more…

www.aaronmullins.com

CONTENTS

PREFACE

The preface for this book will mostly be a list of praise for the people around me. If you're looking for the childhood events and life experiences that inspired each of my stories, I have put them in The Story Behind the Stories section at the end. Got to let you read the secrets before I reveal their source!

Thank you to those of you who still write in a Highland accent on social media, you helped me put together the dialogue spellings for some of my characters – fit's eh crack eh day?

Thank you to my patient and honest proofreaders who have had their phones ping at all times of the day and night with various drafts to look over. To my family and friends, your time and feedback are greatly appreciated. Thank you to all of you who purchased and read my previous work – don't worry, I'm better now.

Most of all, thank you to those that have believed in me since I met them, however long that may have been. My friends, old and new, are always an inspiration to me – particularly for the stranger characters.

Special thanks go to my editorial team – the guys – Christopher, Stuart and Matthew, for the proofreading, research links, endless support and keeping my dialect honest. Thank you, Catherine, for your incredible eye for detail. Thank you, Jodie, for always knowing exactly what is missing. And Ami, for your witty input and unwavering support.

A special mention too for the people I have messaged over the past year or so with really random questions about our home town, the surrounding area and childhood memories – we'll get through therapy together.

Of course, being a conscientious author I need to clarify that, although I use real place names, each story is an obvious work of fiction, with character names and events completely made up. Like all writers, I was inspired by people I have met and events I have seen. But any connection to any real-life person, whether living or dead, is purely coincidental.

With my childhood home town as a reference point, a few of my own adventures and memories may have been a starting point for story ideas. But that's fine. I own the copyright to those.

The stories cover a small range of genres, generally mystery or thriller in nature. Some have a hint of the supernatural about them, a few horror elements. A couple of them represent my first attempt at writing in a new genre – expanding my writing skills, as all authors should. All my proofreaders had a different favourite story, which is always a good sign.

They say write about what you know, which is why I was always going to write a book based in Scotland. I had intended to always be writing something, but my adventures took over – serving in the military, travelling the world, setting up my businesses, gaining a PhD – all fun distractions.

I had served in the RAF and was leaving to go to university. Even though I was majoring in psychology for my undergraduate, I was allowed to choose an elective module. I could have gone for something more academic, but the love of writing from my childhood made my choice for me: Creative Writing.

This was a turning point, rediscovering my passion for writing, as well as studying my craft. It taught me the basics of being an author, which I would then practice every year for the rest of my life so far. I was finally doing what I had intended all along. You can read more of my personal journey in the Author's Notes at the end.

So the only person left to thank is you – for taking the time to read my work. I hope you enjoy it.

Aaron Mullins

www.aaronmullins.com

1: THE ROAD TRIP

Jenny bit her tongue and tightened her grip on the steering wheel. The north coast scenery was stunning, but the steep road she was traversing cut through the notorious Berriedale Braes. An unwelcoming forest to her left and a sheer drop to the North Sea on her right. She held her breath. Her boyfriend, Malcolm, sat in the passenger seat, staring out into the stormy evening sky.

"You love this bit, don't you?" she said, wrinkling her delicate button nose. She risked a glance at him, pouting her full lips and scrunching her gentle blue eyes in mock annoyance.

"Best bit of the trip," he replied with a broad grin.

She enjoyed the annual road trip through the highlands, stopping briefly at Golspie, before heading on to Thurso. As the road levelled off, she blew out a relieved sigh and threw Malcolm a smile.

"So," she said, pushing a long wisp of auburn hair behind her ear. "I have a surprise for you."

"Really?" he asked, raising his eyebrows.

"I thought that instead of staying at our usual places, we could go for something different this time?"

Malcolm nodded, thick brown curls bobbing on his forehead. "Okay, what do you have in mind?"

"Well, remember last year we saw a sign for that bed and breakfast just past Lybster?" she ventured. "If we get a room there we'll have time to visit Whaligoe Steps before we leave tomorrow?"

"Great idea babe," he replied. "What's it called?"

Jenny shook her head. "I don't remember, but it's on the left."

"Okay," he said. "I'll look out for it."

Despite the weather, they marvelled at the scenery as they passed through beautiful villages dotted along the coast. After Malcolm's mother had passed away they had considered cancelling the trip but decided it was more than just a road trip for them, it was therapy. An escape from normality. The break they both needed.

She switched to full beams as the darkened skies brought the night in early. Rain lashed the windscreen and the wipers worked overtime to uncover the path ahead.

"There," shouted Malcolm, pointing at a small sign next to a narrow mud track road. Jenny squinted at the dusk-hidden name buried beneath the branches of overgrown pine trees.

Craigenwind Guest House.

She turned onto the road, darkness swallowing them as the trees enclosed above. After a short drive, they emerged from the canopy into a square patch of overgrown grass. Turning into the make-shift car park, their headlights washed over the exposed stone walls of a two-storey farmhouse. Through the rain, they could see a thick thatched roof. A single light within the building revealed paint peeling from a small arched window.

"Er… looks welcoming," said Malcolm, his tone neutral. He tilted his head to look out the window. A short flagstone path lined with bracken and hogweed lead to a wooden door. Several cars were already parked on the long grass.

"I think that's a Ford Cortina," Malcolm whispered, wiping his sleeve in circles on the window. "1965 model." Jenny pulled up next to it and cut the engine.

"Yes it definitely is a Cortina," said Malcolm, his voice a little louder. "In good condition too."

Jenny smiled. She was used to Malcolm getting excited about old cars and had spent many a weekend walking with him around vintage car rallies.

"And I think I saw a Vauxhall Cavalier over there," he said, releasing his seat belt and turning to peer through the back window. "They haven't made that version since the early 1980s."

"Maybe the owner is a collector," said Jenny with a yawn. She popped her seatbelt off and pointed her toes as she stretched the tiredness from her legs. "Let's hope they have a spare room."

Malcolm leaned over and planted a kiss on her cheek, his deep-set hazel eyes holding a smile.

"Let's do this," he said, zipping his coat and flinging the car door open.

The rain pelted them as they grabbed their bags from the boot and slipped across the wet grass. Avoiding the worst of the moss on the path, they noticed the door was ajar, a soft yellow light emanating from the crack. A bell jangled nearby as they burst through the door, finding themselves next to a small desk in a wide oak-panelled hallway. Beside it stood an over-filled umbrella stand that bulged with a variety of brollies and walking sticks. A pair of hiking poles poked from the top of the pile, their handles hidden beneath a vintage bowler hat. A wooden sign on the desk read 'Reception'.

They closed the door and dropped their bags on the scuffed wooden floor. The hallway smelled of damp wood, the musty odour imbued with a hint of perfume. The sweet scent grew stronger as a short woman with curly grey hair emerged from a doorway behind the desk. Her ornate silver rings scraped on the hard wood as she spread her hands across the desk.

"Fàilte air luchd-siubhail", said the woman, raising a thin finger to slide her spectacles back up her sharply angled nose. "A bheil feum agad air seòmar?"

Jenny looked at Malcolm, who returned her blank stare.

"Um… English?" said Jenny, rubbing a hand on the back of her neck as she met the piercing blue eyes that gazed across the desk.

The woman's smile widened into a crooked grin and she brought her hands together in a single loud clap. "Aye coorse, am Maggie Munro, welcome tae ma hame, dae ye need a room?"

Jenny nodded. "Do you have one spare?"

"Aye," said Maggie. "Twintie quid fur th' nicht."

Malcolm gave a small nod and reached for his wallet.

"We'll take it," said Jenny with a sigh of relief.

"Haur ye go," said Maggie, pulling a key from within the breast pocket of her burgundy blouse and dangling it in front of her. "Room nine. End o' the hall, up th' stairs an' tae th' left."

"Thank you," said Jenny, taking the key as Malcolm placed a twenty pound note on the desk.

"You must have a full house," said Malcolm.

Maggie shook her head. "Yeur th' only guests tonecht."

"But I thought… the cars…" said Malcolm.

"Och, never heed them," said Maggie with a shrug. "They dinnae belang tae anywan."

Malcolm raised his eyebrows. "They're abandoned?"

Maggie's smile faded and she gave a single slow nod.

"Okay, well… we'll go get settled in," said Jenny.

Maggie's tight-lipped grin returned. She watched them in silence, scratching her nose as they carried their bags through the hallway and creaked their way up the stairs. With a click, the door with a hand-painted number nine on it unlocked and opened with a high-pitched squeal.

Jenny flicked the light switch on and went inside. She was greeted by a fresh waft of musty air. A large double bed took up most of the room with a pair of small bedside tables tucked into the corners. Simply decorated, there was an oak wardrobe immediately to their left and a closed red-painted door on their right.

"Well that was weird," said Malcolm, moving into the room and placing his bag on the tartan-carpeted floor. "Bit of an oddball that one."

"Probably doesn't see too many people out here," said Jenny, setting her bag down and walking to the far side of the bed. Avoiding looking into the night, she closed the curtains on the single mullioned window. A small plume of dust tickled her nose as the curtains came together.

"Not fond of cleaning either," said Malcolm, running a finger through a fine layer of dust on the bedside table. For a moment they both stood still, the silence only broken by the beating of the rain on the window.

"We forgot to ask about breakfast," said Jenny.

"If the kitchen is anything like this room…" said

Malcolm, opening the drawer on the bedside table.

"We'll find somewhere nearby in the morning," suggested Jenny. She opened the red door to reveal a narrow bathroom. "I'm going to run a bath before we catch a cold."

As she turned the tap, the clanking and singing of old pipes echoed around the bathroom, eventually spitting its contents out in violent bursts. Popping the plug in, she looked around the room. Two toothbrushes sat in a porcelain cup, a third discarded next to a pair of plain silver earrings resting on a shelf above sink. Open-heeled slippers were tucked beneath the sink, their inner soles yellowed and worn. She stuck her hand into the water. Satisfied with the temperature, she walked back into the bedroom.

"Strange…" said Malcolm, his hand emerging from the drawer clutching two sets of car keys. One of the keys was attached to a Ford Cortina keyring.

Jenny frowned. "Keys but no owners?" she asked. "Maybe she keeps them there in case they come back one day? They seem to have left a few possessions in the bathroom too."

"Maybe," said Malcolm, digging his phone out of his pocket. "But why would they leave them in the first place? I'm going to look this place up on Google."

Jenny shrugged off her wet coat, slinging it on the floor next to her bag.

"Great," said Malcolm, "No internet. No signal either."

"It's the countryside babe," said Jenny walking over to him and helping him remove his jacket. "Let's just try and enjoy the peace and quiet."

"You're right," he said, enfolding her into his arms and kissing her forehead. "Just promise me one thing though, okay?"

"What's that?"

"No more surprises," he chuckled, squeezing her tightly.

"Deal," she laughed, pretending to punch his chest as she released herself from his arms and made her way to the wardrobe. She grabbed their coats off the floor and opened the wardrobe door. Sitting at the bottom of the wardrobe were four pairs of shoes, two men's and two women's. A man's Harrington bomber jacket and a vintage ruffle dress were hanging above them.

"She called this her home," said Jenny, eyeing the clothing. "Do you think her family lives here?"

Malcolm shrugged. "Possibly."

Jenny pushed the items to one side and hung their jackets on spare hangers. She closed the door and wriggled out of her clothing, shivering as the cold enveloped her bare skin.

Steam billowed into the bedroom as she pushed open the red door and went inside.

"At least there's hot water. Feel free to join me," she said with a wink as she closed the bathroom door. She turned the hot tap off, added a little cold and then sank into the soothing warmth of the bathwater. Sighing, she let herself slide down until her ears were fully submerged, then leaned her head back. She closed her eyes and let the ache of the drive seep from her body.

She barely heard the scream.

Water splashed as she jolted upright.

A shout now. Voices arguing, a man and a woman.

Jenny gripped the sides of the bath and listened as the angry voices grew louder. Footsteps followed until the voices were right outside their room.

"Malcolm?" she whisper-shouted.

No reply.

She called again, her voice cracking as she called his name out loud this time.

The bedroom remained silent.

Jenny froze as she heard a key click in a lock and a familiar high-pitched squeal. Somebody had opened the door to their room.

The voices were louder now as the door slammed shut.

"You always do this," shouted a young woman, her speech slurred as if drunk. "It's supposed to be our anniversary."

"You're the one who couldn't keep your eyes off our waiter" a young man shouted back.

"Don't be ridiculous," the woman said. A loud thump and cursing followed.

"Light that candle," the man snapped. "I can't see a thing in here."

Jenny's head swam and she realised she had been holding her breath. She quietly raised herself out of the bath, wishing she had brought fresh clothes in with her. Water pooled on the wooden floor as she reached to grab a towel from next to the sink. Wrapping it around her body, she stepped towards the door and pressed her ear against the wood.

She heard feet shuffling across the carpet.

Her hand trembled as she slid the bolt across to lock the bathroom door, the grate of its closure deafening in the echo of the small bathroom.

"What was that?" said the woman from the other room.

"You're hearing things," said the man. "Pour me another drink."

Footsteps crossed the room. Jenny could hear the

woman's shallow breaths coming from the other side of the door. The handle creaked as it slowly turned, the door straining against the bolt.

"I think there's somebody in there," said the woman.

"Probably the waiter," muttered the man. "Where's my drink?"

"Here," screamed the woman, followed by the sound of smashing glass.

"Oh no…" said the man. "The candle-"

His shout was drowned by the whoosh of air being sucked from the room, followed by the snip-snapping of dry wood caught in a blaze.

Jenny coughed and blinked away stinging tears as smoke poured into the room from beneath the door. She groped for the door bolt, slid it open and fell into a brightly lit room, her knees burning as they slid across the carpeted floor.

"Jenny?" Malcolm looked down at her from the bed. "You okay?"

She stared up at him, eyes wide as she took in the scene. The room was exactly as she had left it.

"There were people… I heard… I thought…" she babbled. Malcolm leapt from the bed and knelt beside her, his arm around her bare shoulders.

"I want to leave," she sobbed.

"Now?" he asked, sensing her urgency. She nodded and scrambled to her feet, pulling her dry clothes out of her bag and dressing hurriedly. She yanked her coat out of the wardrobe, not caring that her wet shoes were already seeping through to her toes.

"I'll drive," said Malcolm. He was standing by the door, bag ready and car keys in hand.

Jenny's heart leapt into her throat as the door squealed

once again. With shaky steps, she crept into the corridor.

Malcolm locked the door with a loud click.

Silence.

Bags slung over their shoulders, every cautious step on the stairs betrayed their exit.

Jenny swallowed, her breath coming in rapid gasps.

Carefully treading along the hallway they realised that Maggie was nowhere to be seen. They left the key on the unmanned desk and peeled the front door open.

The jangle of the bell struck the oak panels lining the hallway walls, carrying its sound deep into the farmhouse.

A door opened upstairs.

Slamming the front door behind them, they rushed to their car and slung their bags into the boot. Malcolm started the engine and Jenny clung to the roof handle as they bounced back down the narrow road. Turning left at the end, they headed north towards Wick. After a short, frantic drive they pulled into the car park of a hotel they had stayed at before.

Jenny's phone pinged twice as it regained signal.

Malcolm pulled his phone out. "Impossible," he said, his mouth hanging open as he stared at the screen. He looked at Jenny, eyes wide as he turned his phone around.

Jenny gasped and her hand rose to cover her mouth. Malcolm's Google search for the guest house had finally gone through and she was staring at an old newspaper article.

Seven Dead in Guest House Blaze.

Jenny's mouth went dry and her chest tightened as she read the article. A fire had swept through the guest house, believed to have been started by a candle in a second floor room. The wooden floors and thatched roof allowed the fire to spread at a rapid pace. There were no survivors.

Amongst the dead were a couple celebrating their anniversary, as well as the owner who lived at the property.

Two photographs accompanied the article. The first showed the burnt remnants of the guest house. Scorched grass and the blackened rubble of the stone walls were all that remained. The second showed a proud owner in front of the guest house on the day it opened. A cold shiver trickled down Jenny's spine. Standing in her burgundy blouse, the piercing blue eyes and crooked grin of Maggie Munro stared straight into her soul.

2: SECRETS OF THE RIVER

The sight of the box filled her with dread, but she couldn't stop touching it. Raindrops cooled and clung to her fingertip as she traced the stag's antlers carved into its centre. Entangled in a briary maze, the creature was surrounded by cruel hounds. A triumphant hunter stood poised to end the chase.

Her finger slipped to the small metal lock bulging from the stag's chest, guarding its secrets. She knew death came for those who sought to open it, but she would be the first to survive. She had stolen the note, and her plan to get the key had begun.

A thunderous crash jolted her from her reverie. Jerking towards the danger, her flailing arm launched salt and pepper pots from her table. They clinked and clattered as they came together and rolled across the café floor.

"We're closing soon," said the waitress, wielding a hard wooden chair onto the adjacent table. She wiped her hands down the front of her apron and grabbed another.

Emily nodded, a glance confirming she was the only

one left. Fighting a shiver, she dug damp tendrils of fine brown hair out of her jacket collar. Her navy wrap dress, speckled near black by her dash through the storm, clung to her ribs as she stretched the numbness from her shoulders. She had to be ready, he would strike soon.

A solitary bell rang from the town hall, marking the half-hour. Its chime drifting above the cars sloshing their way up the street, their waves cresting and breaking against the curb. She had lost track of which hour it partnered, her phone the victim of a rushed escape.

She scanned the walls for a clock, finding only a slew of adornments venerating life in this small Scottish town. Watercolour boats bobbed in the local harbour. Picturesque farms nestled amongst fields of heather rendered forever in bloom. Vintage posters from a local theatre group clambered for top billing amid a fleeting audience. An alluring backdrop to a deadly pursuit.

She massaged the bridge of her nose, pinching away the sleepless nights that lay heavy in her eyes. Her cold coffee sat untouched, its rich aroma long since bittered and died.

It's time to bait the hook.

Trembling, she peered out the café window, squinting into the darkness. Through the driving rain, she could see him standing at the edge of the car park.

Her hunter.

His hands hid in the pockets of his long black coat, blending his tall frame with the growing gloom. He had tilted the brim of his hat forwards, disguising his features in shadow. His large glistening boots pointed accusingly towards her window.

Motionless.

Unperturbed by the rapids dripping past his face. He watched her, like a vulture hunching its dark wings, waiting for the chance to feed.

She shrunk back in her chair, the weight of the hammer concealed beneath her dress pressing into her thigh.

Footsteps.

Her body tensed as the waitress replaced the scattered condiments to their former positions.

"Horrible out there," said the waitress, flipping the sign on the door. Her gaze dropped from the window to the box. "I see you got caught out earlier."

She had.

As she had ripped the muddy box from the river, he had emerged from behind the boating shed, striding across the grass towards her. Caution abandoned and box stuffed inside her coat, she had splashed her way to the path and fled into the stormy street.

Sprinting as fast as she dared, the rain had whipped with cruel intent, threatening to upend every step. Weaving through the streets, a flotilla of umbrellas had masked the annoyance of jostled pedestrians. She leapt puddles too rushed to reflect the troubled sky, her pursuer crashing through her wake.

With a desperate gamble and the blaring of horns, she had burst into a crowded cafe, reaching the safety of the herd. Collapsing into a seat with a view of the road, she had stammered an order and began her vigil.

She had watched him stroll across the street and come to a stop, thwarted but not defeated. She knew he would wait, relentless but patient, he couldn't risk losing his prize. Cracks in the cobbles had filled and flowed and formed as one. Kids splashed and parents pulled. Shoppers hurried home.

Still, he waited.

Crowds had chattered and buzzed around her. Arrivals

breezed against her frigid legs, a second stroke on departure. Time was marked by the sporadic scraping of wooden chairs on the varnished floor and the ever-present rattle of crockery. Anticipation infused with the grating whir of a coffee grinder.

And still, he waited.

The herd had dispersed, like forest birds fleeing before the chase, and she alone now stared up at the waitress. She appeared taller than the girl that had taken her order. Older too, furrows scratched around the edge of deep-set eyes the colour of midnight. Her pale oval face carved strong rather than striking. An uncompromising knot of thick red hair swept back from her forehead. The clipped lilt of an exotic accent infiltrated her speech, delivered with assertive finesse.

"Pretty box. Looks old?"

"It is," Emily whispered, shifting to plant her heels on the floor.

"Is it one of those antique musical ones?" Said the waitress, her height intimidating as she reached across the table.

"No." Emily snatched the box into the crook of her arm, blocking it from inspection. A dull thud echoed from the depths of the table as the hammer slipped off her thigh and hit the chair between her legs. The waitress jumped back, her cheap black slip-ons squeaking with the sudden movement. She stood with folded arms and narrowed glare.

Emily crept a hand below the table and grasped the handle. Rain violently battered the window as she pulled the hammer across her thigh and let it hang by her leg.

Out of sight.

Ready.

She forced down a dry swallow, the box grazing the table as she slid it tight to her chest.

Shadows met and merged outside the window, continuing on their way together. Their voices drowned by the low rumble and hiss of a bus plotting a course through the storm.

"Okay... well, we're closed now so..." said the waitress, lowering her gaze with an apologetic shrug and extending an arm towards the door.

"I need a minute."

"Rough day?"

Emily sighed. "Very. May I use the toilet?"

"Sure, but make it quick. I'm locking up out back, then leaving."

Emily waited until she was alone before rising to her feet, a steadying hand on the table. Her back to the window, she concealed the hammer inside her jacket sleeve. Stomach churning, she gripped the box and crept across the café. Without looking back, she slipped through the door marked 'Ladies'.

Avoiding the mirror, she scurried inside the farther of the two cubicles. Door locked, heart thumping, she perched on the closed toilet lid and placed the box between her feet.

The bait has entered the trap.

A stale cough wracked her throat as she inhaled the synthetic burn of bleached porcelain and cheap air freshener. Withdrawing the damp note from her coat pocket, she gently revealed its message. Yellowed with age and hastily scrawled, the short strokes carried both a dying mans wish and a warning.

'Alistair, I hast failed. I fear e'en now Edward assembles

his might to strike upon our cause. Lord Grey bids us rebels, yet knows not what we guard. We must keep true to our sacred office, protect His relics, now and always. I pray of thou to take this box into thy possession, wheryn lies a most divisive artifact. Encave it where it may ne'r be discovered by those who seek to corrupt its power. Bury the key, for the box shall bid folk to release its prize. It would not doth well for't to fall into the hands of the king. Our congregation shall resist as long as we can. May God watch over us all.

Thy faithful servant – TS.'

She folded the note and returned it to her pocket. Discovering it was written by Thomas Sallow, a reclusive missionary, had been the breakthrough she had needed. The information stolen from the journal of a murderer. The same one that stalked her now.

Afraid for his life as he fought in the rebellion against King Edward VI, Thomas had smuggled his faith's most precious relic to the Scottish Highlands. Alistair Jack, a retired vicar living alone on the banks of Wick River, had become its guardian.

Under torture, Thomas had betrayed his faith and the hunt had begun.

The enthralling enigma of the box had transcended generations. Its inferred powers forming the edifice of shadowy cabals and veiled beliefs. Lain hidden all these years, it became a mystery intensified by imagination, its reward unclaimed.

A countdown that had never reached zero.

The journal tracing its whereabouts had been penned by ruthless narrators. Ownership inherited each time its holder fell in the chase. It held secrets coerced into revelation, evidence extracted by painful means. And a final clue that none had ever solved.

Until today.

A bell tinkled in the cafe.

He had sensed the kill was close. Emboldened by darkness and isolation, he unwittingly played his role.

She reached into her sleeve and removed the hammer.

Wet footsteps grew louder.

She eyed the box, fighting the urge to smash it open and halt her reckless plan. Become the first to glimpse the relic. Brandish the unknown.

A gust of air brushed her ankles as the door opened. A second breath as it closed. A weak thud signalled the end of the chase, like the final beat of a failing heart.

The trap snapped shut.

Silence.

A shadow, edging closer, accompanied by the slippery steps of heavy boots.

Feet halted outside her door, the shadow creeping beneath.

Pulse lurching, she held her breath.

"So you finally figured it out, huh?" he said, his voice cuttingly familiar.

She clenched her teeth and gripped the hammer tighter.

"You know, I searched that river a hundred times."

A cold sweat washed over her courage.

"How'd you do it Em?"

She released her breath, easing the throbbing in her head.

From whispered rumours, she had dug beneath the Grey Cairns of Camster. On borrowed beliefs, she had picked through the ruins of the Castle of Old Wick. Arriving, like those before her, at the lost generations. The trail dark, save for the final anonymous clue - *'it lays entombed within the seat of the foe'*.

"Don't ignore me Em," he said, his voice rising, a cultivated edge of menace sharpening his command. "I ain't mad at you, though I was, of course, when I found you'd tried to steal everything I've worked for. But now... I figure you've done me a favour."

Hard fingers drummed against the door.

"The note was in the chair, wasn't it?"

He was right.

A Scottish box chair, recently acquired by the Heritage Museum. Spoils of war stolen by William Grey. The same Lord Grey sent by King Edward VI to put down a rebellion.

The note had lain there all this time, entombed within the seat of the foe. A clue left behind when the box had been moved to its watery hollow.

"Look Em... Seeing as you've kindly run off and got my box for me, I'll make this easy for you." His mean knuckles requested entry. "Knock... knock..."

She eased and re-clenched her grip on the handle, staving off the growing numbness.

A fist slammed against the door. "C'mon, you know how this ends. We both know—"

"Give me the key."

"The key?" A torturous laugh, excited at the promise of pain. "What makes you think I've got the key?"

"Set it on the floor and leave."

Another cackle, long and cruel. "Give me the box and I'll make it quick."

She had expected this. None of the run-throughs in her head had ended with him handing her the key. Not without a fight.

"Time's up," he said, taking a step back. "This ends now."

She braced her feet and raised the hammer above her head.

The door crashed open, slamming against the cubicle wall.

With a roar, she leapt forwards and swung the hammer. Its wild arc met only air, the sudden momentum dragging her off balance.

She had missed.

Before she had a chance to regain her footing, he grabbed her. Pain exploded in her wrist, slammed against the edge of the sink. A shrill crack ringing out as the hammer fell and clattered across the floor.

Her free hand lashed out, he blocked it.

"It'll never be yours," he snarled, grabbing her from behind and pinning her arms, hours old nicotine breath hot against her ear.

She struggled, feet skidding on the wet floor as they spun in a deadly clinch. An arm slipped up her chest and closed around her throat. Trapped breath suffocated her with the stench of damp cloth.

Dizzy, she fought the choke.

He pulled harder, lifting her to her tiptoes. Her faltering legs flailed against his shins. Wrist burning, she scratched and clawed, fingernails gouging wet fibres, unable to find skin.

A meaty crack.

She fell, the wind knocked from her lungs as his weight sprawled her flat.

Deafened by the rushing of blood, she rolled her torso and pushed his body off her hips. The waitress hovered over her, a marble chopping board lofted in the air, ready to strike again.

Emily's arms begged to let her slip to her elbows.

The waitress lowered her weapon. "You hurt?"

A tight band of pain pulsed from her temples as she nodded. Taking a deep gulp of air, she dragged her legs free, pushing herself onto aching knees.

"Do you know him?"

Ignoring the waitress, she hooked an arm and a leg, rolling him onto his back. Leaning over his body, she rummaged through his coat pocket.

Nothing.

Second pocket.

Empty.

She half unbuttoned his coat and felt for an inside pocket, withdrawing a thin wallet that held only cash. Tossing it aside, she fumbled her way through the rest of the buttons. His chest rose and fell in shallow waves.

Flinging his coat wide open, she patted his trouser pockets. Her hand struck only thigh. Sodden slaps probed the rest of his clothing, hope frisked away palm by palm.

"Where is it?" The question punctuated by fists hammered against his chest.

A firm hand settled on her shoulder. "Shhh, it's ok, he'll be out for a while," said the waitress.

One last check of the pockets, still empty. Her plan had failed.

"What you looking for?"

She sat on her heels and wiped a trembling hand across her forehead. "Nothing."

Her cheeks puffed a long sigh. Staring at the stillness of his face, her jaw tightened. She didn't have the key, but she had survived him. Her search would continue. This time she would be more careful, tread paths he couldn't follow.

She was alive, and she still had the note and the box.

The box.

Terror ripped through her thoughts.

She spun on her knees, twisting to dive back into the cubicle. It sat where she had left it, the stag unmoved, the hunter still poised. The blurry sting of relief accompanied a familiar dread. It called to her, compelling her to face unseen fears and taste forbidden pleasures. She reached out, surrendering herself to its bidding.

Pushing down on the toilet seat, she stood and stumbled out of the cubicle. The waitress leant over his body. Her apron removed, its strings now bound his hands.

Seeing her emerge, the waitress put an arm around her and led her back through the door to the cafe.

"Wait here," said the waitress, lowering Emily into the nearest seat.

"Please," Emily whispered. "No police. Not yet."

The waitress nodded a solemn understanding and disappeared into the kitchen, returning with two mugs of fresh black coffee.

"Will settle the nerves," she said, placing one in front of Emily before taking the seat opposite and sipping from her own. "Popped a little cold in."

The heady aroma awakened a barren thirst, its heat idyllic. Emily gulped a large mouthful, not caring that it burned. Comforting warmth spread through her, a bittersweet caress lingering on her tongue. She closed her eyes, leaned back in the chair and remained motionless for a while. She could hear cars still splashing down roads and rivulets, though fewer now.

"Thank you," Emily said, stretching her legs as she took another long swig. She set the box on her lap and held the mug in both hands, grateful for the soothing heat.

She drained the rest of the coffee with a satisfied sigh. Waves of fatigue washed over her as over-worked muscles finally laid down their arms. Her fingers played over the bumps of the box, tracing a blind path through the maze to stroke the stag, always ending upon the little lock guarding its heart.

"They hung him you know," said the waitress.

The hair on the back of Emily's neck bristled to attention. Her body plunged once again into an icy river, cold and confused. She forced open heavy eyelids. The waitress was staring at the box.

"Wha... you..." Emily slurred, her tongue lolling through a fog of unanswered questions.

"Thomas. In chains, from a church tower. What was left of him anyway," said the waitress, parting a tight-lipped smile. A wildfire of desire consumed her unblinking gaze. "It's beautiful."

Emily let the mug drop to the floor and her loose head tilted forward. Her shaking hands clasped the edge of the table, the box tipping precariously as she drew in her weary legs. All vigour gone, the struggle to remain upright was draining. A smothering effluvium billowed through her mind, hiding memories and concealing thoughts. Defiance lost in its impotent haze.

"When I saw him run after you I guessed you'd found it," said the waitress, pushing her chair back and reaching an arm beneath the table.

Emily succumbed to the numbing waves flooding her body. Her grip failed and her arms fell, dangling at her sides as she slumped in the chair. The back of her skull sank into the ornate groove on the ridge of the chair, arresting her slide. Through the stillness, a hand slipped up her thigh and a weight lifted from her legs.

"He'd become reckless. Easy to follow," said the waitress, her arm emerging from beneath the table with the box. "I watched him day after day blindly scouring that river."

Emily bore silent witness as a rough fingertip ran across the filigree, cutting straight to the ripples of the stag's antlers.

"I prefer the old ways," said the waitress. She tapped the lock and waved a hand over the table, like a magician revealing the grandest of tricks. "Subtlety and subterfuge."

Emily watched the waitress rise and walk out of view. She re-entered a moment later dressed in a dark green quilted jacket, hood pulled tight over her head.

"Though sometimes a blunt approach has its place," said the waitress, nodding towards the toilet door. She threw a thumb over her shoulder towards the kitchen. "And I needed to work this shift more than she did."

One final heavy blink and Emily's sight faded away.

"I knew you didn't have the key," said the waitress, reaching inside Emily's pocket and removing the note. "But I'll take that."

Above the humming and rushing of blood, Emily heard footsteps walking away. The tinkle of a bell, the jangling of keys, then the cold hard snap of a lock. Alone, she waited for sleep to take her.

*

Released from her disguise, the not-a-waitress stepped into the rainy night. As she locked the door, the growl of an engine struck up behind her. Reflected in the glass she saw a large van lurking in the corner of the car park.

Headlights off.

Wipers frantic.

On the pavement opposite a man in a thick bomber jacket and baseball cap shuffled his feet, his focus concentrated on the depths of a darkened window display. His head turned towards her, then flicked away again. His back stiffened and his feet became still. Through the straits and streaks on the glass, their reflected eyes met.

She pressed a palm against the hammer secreted at her waist and slowly turned to face the hounds. Feet firm, she gave a nod to the night.

Rain pelted the box as her finger slipped over the small metal lock in the middle of the stag's chest. She knew death came for those who sought to open it, but she would be the first to survive. She had stolen the note, and her plan to get the key had begun.

3: EQUAL TO AND GREATER THAN

Billy Kendelman killed me in art class.

Not right away, of course. That would be a step too far, even for him.

He was more subtle in his approach to my misery. A deliberately-timed slap on the back as I was balancing a tray of paints with both hands. All 9 pots spaced 3 centimetres apart to form a perfect square. My concentration focused on timing the sloshing of the brimming pots, matching the sway of my stride for the 17 steps needed to return to my seat.

Friendly enough to appear innocent to a teacher's eyes. Hard enough to send me sprawling across my desk. The corner knocked the air from my lungs as the paints splattered my chair, the floor and everything else within reach of the crash site.

The class erupted into jeers and laughter.

I could feel the weight of the paint sliding down my brow, my triangular face encouraging it to race over my cheeks and pool on my thin lips. Spitting paint as I struggled to breathe, I looked around me. The world slid out of focus.

Not again.

I knew there were 22 other people in the classroom, 23 including the teacher, but I couldn't make out individual faces. Their meaningless expressions surrounded me. My chest tightened as their noise crashed over my senses.

Too bright. Too loud.

I closed my eyes and started counting backwards, trying to block out the chaos around me.

10... 9... 8...

I put my hands over my ears, but their strange chatter still seeped through. They spoke to me, but the rules of language escaped my grasp, all meaning lost in a garbled swirl of foreign phonetics and broken grammar.

7... 6...

My fingers tapped out the countdown on the side of my head.

5... 4...

I let the numbers fill my mind, their order comforting.

3... 2...

The pain in my chest eased its grip.

1... 0...

"Alright, settle down," said the teacher, his voice cutting through the noise. His words clear as logic wrest control of my brain once more.

The class quietened down to titters and murmurs.

I was still gasping for breath. Paint dripped from my chin and a chalky metallic taste lingered on my tongue.

"James," said the teacher, calling my name. "Go and get cleaned up."

I steadied myself, opened my eyes and clambered to my feet. I kept my gaze fixed to the floor, my rising embarrassment hidden beneath the paint.

"Freak," whispered Billy as I walked past to leave the classroom.

I counted the 48 steps from the classroom door to the boy's toilets. Greeted by a waft of bleach, I picked my way around the cracks until I reached the sink. The mirror showed my strawberry-blonde hair dyed the colours of the rainbow, my facial palette mixing it in places to match the brown of my eyes.

With a sigh, I turned the tap.

1… 2… 3… 4…

After 5 seconds I stuck my hands into the cold flowing water.

Why did we have to move?

I'm now the youngest boy in my class (11 years, 3 months, 19 weeks and 4 days). It's difficult enough to make friends in a new school, but my 1 in 54 condition was making it even tougher. The 329 miles of change had frightened me. The bigger class sizes were terrifying.

The world scares me.

Once I was old enough to understand, my mother had explained everything to me. Why sometimes I can't find the words to express how I'm feeling. Why crowds of strangers make my skin itch.

Why I was different.

I cupped the water in my hands and splashed it on my face, a refreshing shock of cold that I repeated 9 more times until the water ran clear of paint. The cooling waves slowed my pulse.

My mother had reassured me that she would always be there for me, reminded me that I was loved. She explained that there were kind people in the world, that we would find each other and become less afraid together. That I would not be alone.

And that I had a gift.

I understood why I was different.

But that's not why Billy dislikes me. He hates my gift. The powers it gives me.

Billy was the smartest kid in our maths class, destined to be chosen as the school champion for the Scottish Maths World Cup, a glory he basked in.

Until I arrived.

Numbers were easy for me. Everything could be broken down to a basic mathematical level. Logic and order applied to the chaos of life. I saw how it all came together.

And my brain achieves that faster than most.

Being better than Billy had angered him. Every day he found creative ways to make me miserable, 18 bruises and 27 lost lunches canonical proof of his hatred.

Maybe once he wins he'll stop.

Today was the school Maths Challenge. The competition to determine who would become the school champion, 9 questions, fastest to the right answers would triumph. Without me there to compete, Billy was sure to win.

I wasn't sure I was going to attend anyway. The event took place in the school hall, in front of everybody. Loud and chaotic, I was already exhausted at the thought of being on stage.

Why can't these things just take place in a nice quiet room?

I pulled my jumper off and folded it 4 times before placing it on the floor. I tried to ignore the paint streaks grating on my nerves, making the skin on my forearms crawl.

Breathe.

My hands shot to my ears as the bell rang to signal the end of class. I fell to the floor, leaning my back against the wall, my knees tucked into my chest.

I've missed class.

I stayed like that, frozen in place as the clang of the bell was replaced with footsteps and laughter. The last class of the day was cancelled. Everybody was making their way to the main hall for the competition.

Everybody except me.

I scratched at the skin on my arms through my school shirt as the itching intensified. The tightness in my chest returned.

This wasn't supposed to happen. It's against the rules. I'll go back to class and collect my-

My thoughts were interrupted by the door opening.

A warm smile beamed down at me.

My best friend, Darren.

My only friend.

"Thought you might need these," he said, holding my coat and rucksack.

Darren had seen me like this before. Since the day I arrived he had defended me where he could. He understood me, accepted I had a different way of looking at the world.

"You know he'll win if you don't show up," said Darren, reaching into my rucksack. "And we'll never hear the end of it."

I nodded and smoothed the sleeves of my shirt. I stretched my legs out and took 3 deep breaths.

"And you know you have the power to stop him," said Darren, his hand emerging from my rucksack holding my most treasured possession. My *Psi-Force* comic, volume 1, issue 23, wrapped in a protective cover. Published in

September 1988, it contains the first appearance of Johnny Do, my favourite superhero.

The calming blue of the *Psi-Force* logo strengthened my resolve.

A pyrokinetic superhero, Johhny Do was a mystery. Battling against his inner demons, he never spoke. A silent conflict fought in his mind, that only he truly understood. Some days he was winning, some days he lost control.

He was a 1 in 54.

His enemies called him Dehman Doosha, *The Demon Within*, because his behaviour often seemed strange and chaotic to those around him.

A hero I could relate to.

Johnny was fiercely protective of his friends. He had a gift. He used it to do good in a world he was slowly learning to interact with.

Darren tapped his finger on the front cover.

I stood up and looked him in the eye.

12 – that's how many muscles it takes to smile, and I was using all of them now.

"We can't let the bad guys win," he said, pulling his jumper out of his rucksack and handing it to me. "Every hero needs a sidekick, right?"

Darren reminded me I was more than just a statistic.

I own statistics.

I own fractions, decimals and algebra too. Integers integrated and inductively reasoned.

My X factor to the nth degree. Limitless power.

I had to be my own hero.

I dabbed my face with paper towels, pulled Darren's clean jumper on and tucked my shirt in. Movements precise, my set jaw and narrowed eyes stared back at me from the mirror.

I've got a Maths Challenge to win.

Billy killed me today. The old me, the scared me.

I couldn't always control my feelings and reactions, but when I could, I would choose to be strong. I would choose to do good. Stand up to the bad guys.

Like Johnny Do.

Everybody battles their own demons, but I'm proud to be me.

Darren held the door open for me.

You don't need a lot of friends when you have one true sidekick.

1 in 54, 9 questions, 1 purpose.

Endless possibilities.

I'm not just equal to, I'm greater than.

I have a gift, and I'm going to use it.

4: THE GALA QUEEN

I knew it was a mistake as soon as I heard her scream, its shrill pitch ringing above the blare of the car horn. The desperate screeching of tyres, then her terrified shriek cut short beneath the violent crunching of metal.

The stench of burnt rubber and spilled petrol hit my nostrils. Jaw hanging open, I retched as the bitter smack of smoke settled on my tongue.

She's gone.

The realisation shook my body with a deep sob, setting off a wracking cough as the smoke burned my throat.

I've got to get out of here.

Hands trembling, I pulled my trousers up and ran.

*

I lay on my bed, the taste of charcoal still souring my tongue, despite brushing my teeth three times. I had hidden my clothes, scrunched and buried at the bottom of the washing basket. My skin tingled from the heat of the

33

shower and the roughness of scrubbing away smells that lingered deep inside my pores.

It was just a prank.

We had done it many times before. At night we would wait until we heard a car approaching and then show our butts at the end of the alley. The shape of the road meant that the car would swing around the corner, their headlights washing over the entrance to the alley, revealing the full moon.

Kids having harmless fun.

It was just one of the many stupid things we did to entertain ourselves. We would dare each other to do more and more outrageous things, but never anything truly dangerous.

And I never turn down a dare. I have a reputation to keep. Craig Macallister, the crazy one.

Tonight wasn't a dare though. There wasn't even anybody to impress. It was just me. Alone on Halloween.

Too old to dress up and go trick or treating.

But not too old to play a few pranks.

I had run out of eggs, having splattered them upon windows across the town. Walking with a triumphant swagger as I made my way home, I cut through the alley that lead to the park. That's when I decided that I had one more trick to play.

A car was approaching.

I yanked my hood up and my trousers down.

Bent over, I glanced to my right. That was when I saw her. A girl heading my way, her white dress and sparkling wings disguising her as an angel. A full bag of treats swung by her side and she was picking the clear wrapper from a toffee apple.

She hadn't seen me.

The car was upon us now, too late to back out. I watched in horror as the girl stepped from the pavement to cross the road, her head down, attention wrapped on unravelling her treat.

Until she looked my way.

And screamed.

I pulled the duvet covers over my head and buried my face in my pillow to hide the sound of my tears. I knew I shouldn't have run away, but there was nothing else I could do.

A single thought kept repeating itself as exhaustion dragged me into a fitful sleep filled with blaring horns and dying angels.

She was gone.

*

Still in my pyjamas, I crept down the stairs and pressed my ear to the living room door. Above the muffled voice coming from the radio, I heard my parents talking.

"It's terrible," said my mother, her voice soft and fragile. "She was so young."

"Old Bobby McClean too," replied my father. "He's in intensive care, his car's a write-off."

I closed my eyes and held a clammy palm over my mouth, fighting the rising sickness in my throat.

"The police aren't looking for anyone else in connection with the incident, but are asking for any witnesses to come forward," said the woman on the radio.

I wrapped my arms around my body, trying to stop the shaking that had taken hold of me.

A girl had died and a man was in hospital because of me.

The thud of my heartbeat drummed loud and fast inside my head.

But they don't know I was there.

I slowed my breathing, opened the door and walked into the living room. My mother rushed to squeeze me, blinking away the tears in her eyes. My father looked up from his newspaper.

"Schools cancelled today honey," she said. "There's been an accident. Do you know a girl called Gemma Larnach?"

I nodded and looked at the floor, gripping onto my mother to hold myself up.

Gemma was in the year below me. A quiet girl, she lived a few roads over. Her brother Ryan was in my class.

"She was knocked down crossing the road last night," said my mother, her voice breaking. "Sadly she passed away."

I couldn't find the words to respond to her. I just stood there, muscles frozen in place, clinging to my mother.

"You don't look well," said my father, peering over the top of his spectacles.

"You're sweating," said my mother, breaking my hold and placing a hand on my forehead. "Burning up… and you've got the shivers too. Back to bed and I'll bring you some breakfast up."

I moved my heavy legs out the door and willed them up the stairs.

I collapsed onto my bed and crawled back under the duvet.

Dead because of me. And nobody knows.

I cried then, for both Gemma and myself. Great tremors of grief coursed through my body in uncontrollable waves of sadness and disbelief.

A painful mix of regret and relief.

I killed her… but I'd gotten away with it.

*

I looked out at the warm summers evening. Nine months had passed since the accident. Bobby McClean had recovered but had no memory of what happened that night. Most of the school and my parents had attended Gemma's funeral, but I had stayed away, said I was too ill to go.

Life had moved on.

It was difficult at first. Ryan had eventually returned to class and I had stuttered a few awkward words of consolation along with everybody else. Christmas had come and gone in a draining blur. But by spring I had stopped having nightmares and when the summer holidays arrived the town was buzzing for warmer days and lighter nights. I was ready to carry on.

No point in two lives being ruined.

Today was a celebration. It was the town gala day. The brightly decorated floats would be travelling through the streets, collecting money to support local causes. Everybody would be out in the sunshine, the whole community coming together for an evening of fun.

From my window, I could see people already lining the streets. I had saved my copper coins to put into the charity tins and was ready to join the festivities.

With a smile, I left the house and made my way towards the town centre. I found a spot with a great view of the street, just in time, as people dressed in a variety of costumes were walking ahead of the first float.

A great wave of music and cheers washed over me as the

float went by. It was decorated to be a pirate ship, with eye-patched men and scantily-clad women shaking cutlasses and collection buckets.

I laughed as a few of my wayward pennies landed and rolled about the deck. More costumed collectors waved to the crowd as they followed in its wake.

A girl wearing a ragged white dress danced along the centre of the street, in and out of the other collectors. Her costume billowed outwards as she spun on the spot. Her face was covered by a featureless red mask with two small holes for eyes. I chuckled and clapped hard to applaud her efforts, though the rest of the crowd appeared not to notice.

Probably because she doesn't have a collection bucket for them to aim at.

She pirouetted and pranced her way down the road until she was in front of me. Coming to a graceful stop, she bowed her head once and then raised a hand, beckoning me over.

I held out a coin, but she shook her head and motioned for me to join her.

I put my coin bag in my pocket and glanced up the road. The next float was far enough away for me to have one quick dance.

I looked back to the street and the girl was now beside the crowd on the opposite side of the road. Nobody paid her any attention as she looked over her shoulder, waved for me to follow and then slipped between a pair of revellers.

A trickle of excitement ran through me as I realised a girl had just asked me to join her for a secret dance. This kind of thing didn't happen to me.

Oh well, here goes.

I checked again that the next float was still a safe distance away, before rushing into the road. I barged my way past the same couple the girl had, though with greater annoyance on their part.

Emerging on the other side, I heard a giggle and glimpsed her waving to me from the end of a short alley that cut between the shops.

"Hey, wait up," I said with a grin and a wave. As I stepped into the alley she raised a delicate hand to her red mask, blew me a kiss and disappeared around the corner.

I licked my hand and pressed my fringe into place before sprinting after her.

When I reached the end of the alley, I turned the same corner and was greeted with an empty street. I looked in the other direction, but there wasn't a soul in sight. No footsteps. The street was silent.

She was gone.

What a strange trick to play.

I walked back towards the cheering crowd. One of the floats must have had a smoke machine because the top of the alley was filled with billowing wisps of white fog. The heady smell of burning incense lay thick in the air as I walked through the plumes of smoke and pushed my way to the front of the hazy crowd.

I could hear a flute playing and the fog eased enough to reveal a procession of dancers. They marched down the road, their footsteps in unison, each holding a deadly weapon. At their head was a tall man playing a mournful tune on a wooden flute. Dressed in grey rags, his leathery black mask covered his entire head, with holes only for the eyes and mouth.

As he drew closer the tune changed, becoming lively, and the dancers broke formation to perform audacious flips and wild leaps. Their frayed outfits matched the flute player and each wore the face of a different animal. Their chaotic costumes whipped the air as they contorted their bodies into unnatural shapes. Hunched bears and pouncing wolves swung axes and sickles with reckless abandon, weaving amid creatures he couldn't even name.

She must have been part of this group.

I froze as the crowd opposite was suddenly revealed by the retreating fog.

Everybody was dressed in long brown robes. Every face was covered by a black mask with a long bird-like beak.

What the-

My head darted left and right.

Everyone around me wore the same costume, their eyes sunk within black pools, hidden deep within the mask. Their muffled cheers echoed from small holes below their beaks.

I tried to push my way through the crowd towards the alley, but they closed the gap, their robed bodies barring the way. They pressed against me, a writhing mass that edged forwards until I was forced into the road.

The music stopped playing.

I looked up the street. The dancers were still. The crowd had gone silent. A cold shiver stood my hair on end as I realised all eyes were turned on me.

W- What's going on?

A single float was coming down the street, creaking as it rolled on giant wooden wheels. Resembling a large cart, the float was pulled by two enormous horses draped in black barding. Upon the float stood a single figure wearing an antler crown, a burning torch held aloft. The orange glow flickered off her featureless red mask and ragged white dress.

It's her.

The dancers moved to the side of the road. Whispered threats passed through the crowd. Their voices rose as the cart rolled closer, snippets of conversation snatched from the air.

The queen comes. Murderer.

The cart halted with an unspoken command. With a graceful flourish, the girl leapt onto the road. She handed her torch to a vulture-headed dancer and then turned to face me. The crowd were roaring now, shoving and jigging and howling with delight.

Killer. Revenge. Life for a life.

I gasped as the crowd ripped off their masks to reveal the grotesque faces of snarling demons and hideous ghouls. Every head bore the nightmarish imitation of a vicious animal. Their twisted features and the stench of their filthy hides caused me to gag. Wet gargles and unearthly shrieks battered my ears, all pretence of humanity stripped from their braying screech.

As the girl walked towards me, I found I was unable to move, my taut muscles trapping me in the middle of the road. Eyes wide, a struggled wheeze escaped my constricted throat.

Pain. Our queen. Slaughter.

I winced as something hard struck me in the face, shocking me loose.

It hit the road with a metallic clink.

I looked down to see an old copper coin, the portrait of a grinning devil etched onto its side. I cried out as the sharp edge of another stung my ear. A third cut into the back of my head.

I crouched and threw my hands over my head as I was pelted with coins. The tinkling grew into a torrent of metal

41

rain that beat against me before amassing on the road.

"Stop… please," I yelled, my hands and body aching from the strikes.

The jeers and laughter were deafening now.

Cut him. Burn him. Make him pay.

The assault suddenly stopped.

I heard a dainty footstep crunch against the pile of coins in front of me.

I opened my eyes.

The girl was towering over my hunched body, her cold dead eyes piercing from beneath her red mask. Up close, I realised that her ragged dress was the torn remnants of a different costume. One that still had the ends of broken wings poking from behind her back.

My chest tightened with a painful gasp as I realised it was the costume that Gemma had worn on the night she died.

Feast on his flesh. Our queen. Tear him apart.

The hysteria of the crowd had driven them into a wild crescendo. Horns clattered against scaled heads, and hooves stomped a terrible beat. Their fiendish cries and blasphemous cackles rang with madness as they shoved against each other, spilling into the street.

A thunderous crash to my left drew my attention. An alligator-headed reveller had bitten a large chunk from the neck of a neighbouring ghoul. Blood splattered the frenzied mob as they fell onto the road in a wild tangle of tooth and claw.

A thought struck me as I stared at the void left behind by the brawling creatures.

I can see the alley.

Flooded with hope, I turned my crouch into a sprinter's start and dashed towards the gap.

My foot lurched on the slippery coins, threatening to plunge me to the ground. Throwing my arms out to prevent my fall, I regained my balance and burst into the crowd.

A claw raked my shoulder, hooking my jumper.

I pulled hard, struggling against it.

A sudden snap and I was thrust forwards again, racing down the alley. Chased by hissing snarls and angry curses, I didn't dare look back.

I exploded out the end of the alley, straight into the deafening blare of a car horn.

*

"He- well- he came from nowhere," said the driver as he ran a shaking hand over his head. "Didn't have a chance to stop."

The police officer noted it down.

"Is he-," said the driver. "I mean- he was still breathing, right?"

"He'll live, but it'll take some time to heal," said the police officer. "As for you, you're free to go. We already know you weren't to blame."

"Really?" said the driver, his eyes wide with relief. "How?"

"He's confessed," said the police officer. "Keeps repeating 'it was my fault' over and over again."

5: REVENGE OF THE GREEN MAN

"He's nicked it," said Charlie, slamming his fist onto the kitchen counter. "It wis sittin' right here."

"Fit's he nicked?" replied Jamie, wincing as he took a sip of his whisky. He coughed as the alcohol caught the back of his throat, causing his large, black-rimmed glasses to fall to the floor.

"Ma Morning Glory CD 'at's whit," shouted Charlie, his beady eyes gleaming with an accusatory glare. "He disny even hev a fucking CD player, still tapes shite aff eh radio. It's 1995 min, he needs til get wi' eh times."

"Och, mibbe he's set it somewhere?" said Jamie, slapping his palms against the sides of his shaved head a couple of times. He picked his glasses up, wiped the lenses on his hoodie and put them back on.

Charlie spun on his heels to face his friend, his thin angular features as red as his hair. "Listen til whit am tellin' ye. He had it in his grottie wee hands, noo he's gone n' eh CD is gone n'all. Av searched 'is hoose tap t'bottom."

Jamie set his empty glass onto the counter and let out a

44

deep burp. "Are ye sure Laura's no' took it? She leks t'borro' stuff."

"Nae chance. Chloe wis at her drama club 'is morning. They went straight til her sisters fo' eh night."

"Whit aboot-"

"It only came oot last week," said Charlie, his skinny frame swaying as he poured himself another drink. "Selt eh cat t'buy it."

"Pussy Galore?"

"Aye, selt her til mad wee Davie fae Dunbeath."

"Davie wi' eh wan eye?"

Charlie nodded and took a long swig of his drink, sloshing it down his pointed chin as he walked through to the living room. "If Laura says any'hing, ye hevny seen her."

"Whit th'fuck's he gunna dae wi' a cat?" said Jamie, moving to take a seat on the sofa.

"More importantly," said Charlie, his eyes shining as he sat next to his friend. "Fit am a gunna dae aboot Big Donny Mackay nicking ma CD?"

"Ye could always gi' 'im a call n' ask if he's got it?"

"And how d'ye think 'at's gunna work oot?" said Charlie. "Naw, there's only wan thing fur it."

"Steal it back?"

"Windaes," said Charlie, yellowed rows of wonky teeth revealing themselves in a wicked grin.

"Windaes?"

"Aye," said Charlie. "Am gunna put his windae through."

"Why?"

"Are ye daft? Fo' revenge Jamie," said Charlie. "Mibbe scare 'im a wee bit, let 'im ken who he's messing wi'."

"Aye cos nothing instils terror lek a draughty living

room," said Jamie, rolling his eyes. "Am sure he'll be straight roond in eh morning wi a scarf on begging fo' mercy."

"It's eh Heelan way," said Charlie, throwing his arms in the air, splattering his drink across the curtains. "Or mibbe a could set his bins on fire?"

"When he finds oot it's ye he's gunna batter-"

"But he's no' gunna ken it's us," said Charlie, knocking back the dregs of his drink as he jumped up from the sofa.

"Us?"

"Aye Jamie, us," said Charlie. "He's robbed us both o' oor Saturday night tunes."

"Am no' bothered t'be honest. Did ye tape Gladiators? We could watch-"

"Get yer coat on," said Charlie.

"Och, c'mon min, jus' sit doon."

Charlie yanked the zip on his parka. "Dinny mek me-"

"Fine," Jamie sighed, finishing his drink and reaching for his trainers. A couple of minutes later they pulled their hoods up and slipped into the dark October evening. Charlie set a brisk pace, his arms swinging with mad intent as he marched to the end of the street. They crossed over and cut down an alley that lead to the park.

"Did ye bring a brick?" asked Jamie, his arms flapping as they made their way across the slippery grass.

"Ah shite."

"We should go back."

"A'll kick his lamppost oot instead."

"Naturally," whispered Jamie to himself. The edge of the park emerged onto a short street. There was nobody else about as they crept towards the pavement.

Suddenly Jamie was yanked behind a tree.

""At's his hoose," whispered Charlie, pointing at a

dimly lit white door across the road.

"Aye a ken 'at ye daft bat, we've both been there a hunner times before."

"Sshhh keep yer voice doon."

"He canny hear us. Or even see us. D'ye ken why?"

"Why?"

"Cos his name's no' Donny Big Lugs n' he disny hev a fucking lamppost ootside his hoose."

"Ah shite," said Charlie, kicking the tree. "A bet he's fucking' Wonderwallin' in there reit noo n'all."

"Jus' go knock on his door n' ask fur it back," said Jamie.

Charlie stood still, his eyes focused on the soft orange glow emanating from behind the drawn curtains of the living room window.

"Fuck 'is," said Charlie. "Watch ma back."

Jamie watched as Charlie raced across the road, leapt the garden wall and disappeared into the darkness on the other side. Hesitating for a moment, Jamie hurried across the road and crouched low before peering over the wall.

"Charlie?"

"Am here," Charlie grunted. A wet bubbling sound drifted up from the other side of the wall.

"Fit's 'at smell?"

"Eh sweet smell o' revenge," whispered Charlie.

"Are ye heving a fucking shite in his garden?"

"Sshhh."

"Fur fuck sake, pull yer pants up min."

"Nearly done."

"Ye said watch yer back, no watch ye tek a fucking shite. I didny sign up fur this."

A high-pitched squeak was followed by another wet rumble.

"Jeez ye're no weel min, ye need t'finish up. How're ye gunna look yer daughter in eh eye n' tell her ye got arrested fur heving yer wonderballs oot in another chiel's garden?"

A tiny puff of gas, then silence.

"Jamie?"

"Aye?"

"Gi' me a dock leaf."

"Where th'fuck am a meant t'get a dock leaf?"

Jamie ducked as a large shadow passed behind the curtains. A moment later he peered over the wall again. Charlie's track suit bottoms and underwear were still around his ankles. He was sitting with his hands between his legs, shuffling across the grass.

"Fit ye daeing noo?"

"Improvising," whispered Charlie, awkwardly sliding his arse further along the lawn.

"We need t'get oot o' here. Whit if a neighbour sees ye? They'll be scouring eh streets looking fur a mad bastert wi' worms."

Charlie slipped off a trainer and removed a sock. Jamie turned away, hoping to avoid seeing things that would haunt his dreams. A few moments later Charlie landed beside him.

"Done?" asked Jamie.

"Aye, but av got an even better idea. Follow me."

*

"Lemme get 'is reit," said Jamie, sinking into the sofa before knocking back a shot of whisky. "Ye wan' us til go tae Dunnett Forest th'night?"

"Aye."

"Tae intercept Big Donny Mackay as he walks his wee

48

dug?"

"Aye again," coughed Charlie, downing his drink before pouring another.

"Dressed as a tree man, lek summat oot o' Lord o' eh Rings?"

"Ah no' jus' any tree man," said Charlie, wagging his finger. "The Green Man."

"And ye ken he's gunna be there how?"

"Cos he always walks wee Alfie at eh same time every night. I even ken whit route he'll tek, walked it wi' him a couple times."

"And how d'ye plan on becoming 'is Green Man?"

Charlie smiled, stood up and ran up the stairs. Jamie lay back on the sofa, listening to the thumps and crashes resounding through the ceiling. He was starting to nod off when Charlie's footsteps stomped back down the stairs.

"Whit d'ye think?" asked Charlie.

"A think ye need new hobbies min," said Jamie, shaking his head. "Is 'at Laura's skirt?"

"Aye," said Charlie, twirling to give Jamie a better look at his full outfit. He was wearing dark green tights on his legs and arms, scavenged from his Ninja Turtles outfit for Halloween. He had cut the feet off one pair to poke his hands through and now wore the remnants over his head as a makeshift mask. On top of this, he had placed a huge brown wig, the back-combed frizzy hair erupting in every direction. The edge of a green t-shirt poked out from the bottom of a black bodywarmer. Laura's black mini skirt, unzipped to fit his waist, completed the look.

"How th'fuck did ye even get 'at on?"

"Never mind 'at," said Charlie, his mouth moving beneath the tights. "Dae I look lek eh Green Man?"

"You look lek a zombie Tina Turner."

"A'll grab some leaves once we're oot there, mek it more authentic."

"And how exactly are we gunna get til Dunnett Forest?"

"Eh same way a girl gets anywhere in 'is toon," said Charlie, hitching up his skirt. "Am gunna stick a leg oot."

*

"It's freezing," said Jamie, shuffling from one foot to the other as they stood at the bus shelter.

"We willny hev t'wait long on a Saturday night," replied Charlie, peering up the road. "In fact, a think a can hear oor chariot arriving noo."

They heard the car before they saw it, the aggressive revving of its engine announcing its arrival long before its headlights swung round the corner. Charlie coyly turned his head away, raised his skirt a bit and lifted one green-tighted leg into the road.

The car swerved as it slowed. Pulling up into the bus stop, the window wound down, revealing the eager faces of two young guys in the front of the car.

"Fancy a wee cruise sweetheart?" said the driver.

Charlie swung his head round, revealing his masked face. "Aye, a dae Bobby."

"Holy fuck min," said Bobby, his eyes wide as he jumped back in fright. "Whit kinda weird shite is 'is?"

"Dae ye no' recognise me, Bobby, it's me, Charlie."

"Why th'fuck are ye dressed lek Tina Turner? asked Bobby, leaning out his window now to take in Charlie's full outfit. "Ye're a bit early fur Halloween."

"Am no' fucking Tina Turner, am eh Green Man. An' it's a private party, but we need a lift. Can ye drop us aff at

Dunnett Forest?" asked Charlie.

"You'se are going til Dunnett Forest, tae a private party, dressed as Tina Turner n' Spud fae Trainspotting?"

"Er… actually… am no' dressed up…" said Jamie, pushing his large glasses back up his nose.

"Let's go," said Charlie, opening the back door. Jamie sighed and climbed in beside him.

*

"Wis 'at an owl?" asked Jamie, his eyes darting back and forth in the dark. "A hope it wis an owl."

Bobby had dropped them off at Dunnett Forest car park and they had made their way along the flattened grass path. It was pitch black, but Charlie seemed to know where he was going. Eventually, they stepped off the path and walked a short distance into the forest. Jamie had lost track of how long they had lain in wait, perched on the soft ground behind some bushes.

"Whit kinda noise d'ye think eh Green Man meks?" asked Charlie. "Lek, d'ye think it's a deep voice full o' wisdom? Or jus' animal noises, lek eh call o' a bird?"

"Hev ye eaten a patch o' mushrooms since we got here?"

"Cooo cooo caaaaw."

"Stop 'at ye daft bastard."

"Yaaaarrrrg."

"Ye've lost yer fucking marbles min."

"Wait… whit wis 'at?" said Charlie.

"Probably a fox come t'shag yer leg cos ye sounded lek-" said Jamie, suddenly stopping as the sharp snapping of wood rang out into the night. They both jumped into a crouch and peered into the darkness. Through the bushes, they saw the faint swish of torchlight raking back and forth over the path. The black silhouette of a small dog ran ahead of its owner.

"It's him," whispered Charlie with glee. "A telt ye he'd come."

Stifling a giggle Charlie adjusted his skirt and edged forwards, ready to pounce. The torchlight came closer, footsteps louder now as the silhouette grew larger.

"Eh Green Man has come fur ye, thief," whispered Charlie.

The dog had reached the bushes they were crouched behind.

Closely followed by its owner.

With a screech, Charlie burst from the trees and leapt into their path. Gyrating his hips, he beat his chest as he yelled with primal abandon.

A woman's startled scream rang out.

"Oh fuck…" whispered Jamie.

The dog snarled and pounced on Charlie, its teeth tearing at his green tights.

"Harold," yelled the woman. "Help."

Jamie turned to see a second torchlit silhouette charging at them from the direction of the car park. Frozen with fear, he nearly tumbled as Charlie burst past him.

"Run," yelled Charlie.

Jamie looked back to see the dog shredding a large wig. He screwed his eyes shut as the torch suddenly swung up to his face.

"In there," shouted the woman, pointing at the bush Jamie was hiding in. "A swear tae God it wis Tina Turner."

"Am eh fucking Green Man," came Charlie's cry from the depths of the forest. Jolted to action, Jamie turned on his heels and sprinted after his friend.

*

"Woulda been a strange way t'die," yawned Jamie, his feet aching as they finally turned onto Charlie's street. They had eventually stopped running and waited long enough for their hunters to give up and go home. Then they had made their way towards the sound of the sea, stumbling back onto the main road near Dunnett Beach. Charlie had been silent for most of the long walk home.

"Mind if a crash?" asked Jamie.

Charlie sighed. "Aye."

They made their way inside. Charlie kicked off his muddy trainers and let the mini skirt fall to the floor. They collapsed side by side onto the sofa.

"'At wis some night," said Jamie. "A need a drink."

"Aye pour me wan n'all," said Charlie. Jamie got up and went through to the kitchen. Grabbing some fresh glasses, he poured two whiskies. Stomach rumbling, he opened the fridge. Suddenly he paused.

"Charlie?" he yelled.

"Aye?"

"C'mere."

Charlie appeared at the door. "Whit?"

"Did ye eat some o' 'is cake before a got here earlier?"

"Aye, whit aboot it?"

"Whit-a-fuckin-boot-it indeed," said Jamie, reaching into the fridge. His hand emerged holding a chocolate-smudged Oasis album. "It wis here eh hail fucking time ye daft bastert."

Charlie's jaw hung open as he stared at the CD, his movements slow as Jamie handed him a drink.

Three loud bangs on the door startled them both.

"Who th'fuck's knocking at eh door at 'is time?" asked Jamie as he moved past Charlie to look out the living room window. "Ah fuck. We're deid."

"Who is it?"

"It's Big Donny Mackay," said Jamie, his head falling into his hands. "An' he's helding a shitey sock."

6: THE HOUSE ON LOVERS' LANE

"And then the witch pulled the horse's tail off," said Lyndsay, her eyes wide as she mimicked yanking an invisible tail. "But Tam escaped because the witches couldn't cross running water."

Cheriee threw her head back and laughed, applauding the tipsy embellishments Lyndsay had added to the story.

"Scary stuff," said Lyndsay, plonking herself onto the damp grass.

"Was a night he'll not forget in a hurry."

"Or the poor horse. I wonder why witches are scared of water?"

"I don't believe in all that supernatural nonsense," said Cheriee, zipping her hoodie as she straightened her back. "There's enough horror in the real world."

"You mean…" said Lyndsay, raising her eyebrows.

Cheriee nodded.

"It's sad," said Lyndsay, a cold shiver trickling down her spine. Hours had passed since they had marvelled at the sunset over the river and the night had unveiled a bitter edge. She drew her knees to her chest and wrapped her arms around them. Casually dressed in jeans and hoodies, neither of them had thought to bring a coat.

"Do you think they'll find him?" asked Cheriee.

Lyndsay propped her chin on her knees. "I hope so."

This kind of thing shouldn't happen in our town.

"It's been a week now…" said Cheriee, the unspoken implication hanging heavy in the crisp night air. They both knew it was becoming less likely that the boy would be found alive. The entire town was on edge, hoping for a breakthrough, but being driven mad by that very same hope.

And suspicion. Everybody watching what everyone else is doing.

The tense atmosphere had become stifling, so they had sneaked out. Told their parents they were sleeping at each other's houses so they could have a break from the blanket of mistrust that lay across the town.

Have some fun.

They had acquired four large bottles of peach-flavoured alcohol, two of which lay empty on the grass, glinting when the moonlight pierced the clouds. They planned to spend the night relaxing in a field next to the riverside, sipping their drinks and telling ghost stories.

A hungry howl screeched from the darkness.

Cheriee scrambled to her feet with a startled cry, causing Lyndsay to laugh.

"It's only Buddy," said Lyndsay, digging into her pocket to reveal an egg-shaped keyring. "He's just letting me know he needs feeding."

Lyndsay pressed a button and was rewarded with the contented yapping of a small dog.

"I can't believe you still have one of those," said

Cheriee, tugging at the edges of her hoodie as she sat back down. "We're sixteen now, we're mature adults."

"Class of '97," said Lyndsay, grabbing an unopened bottle and waving it in the air.

"Sshh," said Cheriee, giggling as she reached for the other bottle. The field they had chosen was at the end of a row of houses. A lovers' lane ran alongside the field, joining the houses with the riverside. It was usually quiet, especially at this late hour, but they still had to be careful.

"Buddy has been alive for 93 days now," said Lyndsay, nuzzling the keyring against her cheek. "I'm his mumma. He needs me."

Cheriee shook her head. "Let's do something to keep us awake," she said through a yawn.

"Truth or dare?" suggested Lyndsay, stuffing the keyring into her pocket and zipping it closed.

"Okay. Truth."

"Do you fancy the guy from the wine shop?" asked Lyndsay, her face broadening into a cheeky grin.

"No way," exclaimed Cheriee, louder than she meant to.

"He looks like Ronan Keating."

"More like Ace Ventura with that shirt," said Cheriee. "Plus, the way you were flirting with him I thought you wanted him to paint you like one of his French girls."

"Well one of us had to secure the goods," said Lyndsay, thrusting her arm out and shaking her bottle. "It worked didn't it."

Cheriee snorted with laughter, which set them both off in a fit of breathless giggles. They each tried to hush the other, which only made them laugh even harder.

Regaining control, they wiped their eyes and steadied their breathing.

"At least he smells nice," said Lyndsay. "A bit of snog fodder?"

"He wears too much Joop."

"No such thing," said Lyndsay with a sigh.

"I was drunk off the fumes before we even left the shop."

Lyndsay threw her hands up in a W symbol. "Whatever. My turn. I choose dare."

"Alrighty then Ventura lover, let's see how brave you really are," said Cheriee, with a devilish smile. "I dare you to do the 'phantom caller'."

Lyndsay covered her mouth with her hand. "Now?"

"Yes now."

"What if somebody's home?"

Cheriee chuckled. "You'd better be careful then."

"You're evil, you know that?" said Lyndsay, climbing to her feet and gazing across the field. The house at the end was a black silhouette against the night sky.

The 'phantom caller' was a game they made up the last time they were here with Claire and Donna. The aim was to sneak through the garden of the house at the top of lovers' lane and touch the door, without setting off the security light guarding the way.

Only one of them had succeeded.

Claire had spent twenty minutes silently rolling across the grass when a faint knock was heard. As she stood and struck a winner's pose, the security light came on. She had raced across the grass and jumped over the fence, a triumphant grin on her muddy face.

And she's reminded us about it every day since.

Nobody had appeared to warn them off. There was no car on the driveway and the house was always in total darkness. They assumed it was abandoned, with the security light to scare off potential burglars.

But attract phantom callers.

Cheriee walked with Lyndsay to the edge of the field.

"If I don't make it," whispered Lyndsay, hopping over the low wooden fence at the end of the garden. "Find Buddy a good home."

She landed in a crouch, paused, and then lowered herself onto her stomach. The grass tickled her nose and poked at her eyes. She flattened the patch in front of her, releasing the earthy scent of rain-soaked soil. The coolness of the damp grass seeped through her jeans.

Better hurry this up.

Pushing from her elbows and knees, she crawled through the long grass. With careful movements, she made steady progress.

I think I'm further than last time.

She risked looking up.

The house was still draped in darkness, the dull yellow glow of the nearby lamppost struggling to penetrate its depths. From her low angle, the windows amplified the overcast sky.

Across the field, an owl hooted. She focused ahead and carried on.

Her elbow landed on hard stone.

Yes.

She smirked in the darkness, her fingers digging into the palms of her hand as she fought the urge to pump them into the air.

Sorry, Claire, it's time to share those bragging rights.

She had reached the narrow stone path that ran alongside the house. All she had to do was sneak past the living room window and knock on the door.

So close.

She turned her head and looked for Cheriee.

The silhouette of an arm rose from behind the fence, thumb pointing upwards.

With a grunt, Lyndsay dragged herself onto the hard path and rose into a crouch, her back pressed flat against the wall. She rubbed her palms on her hoodie and sucked in deep breaths, glad to be off her stomach.

Here goes.

She lowered herself to her hands and knees and crawled along the path. She paused beneath the large window and sat back on her heels to give her pained knees a rest from the hard stone.

Before she could set off again, a faint weeping drifted to her ear.

She froze.

Holding her breath, she peered across the dark garden as she listened to the night.

Another pained whimper crept into the air.

It's coming from the house.

She turned to stare at the window above her head. Reaching her arm up, her fingers gripped the rough edge of the window ledge. She tightened her jaw and lifted her head.

What the…

As she rose a weak orange glow revealed itself in the centre of the ledge. The tiny sliver of light was leaking from a small gap in the bottom of the curtains.

Her heart raced as her shaking hands raised her body just enough to peer through the window.

Please don't be-

Her stomach swooped as she stared at the source of the crying.

Oh my God, it's him.

A small candle flickered on a battered coffee table, its meagre light catching a boy slumped on a wooden chair. His thin feet and frail hands were bound to the chair. A frayed rag covered his mouth and his body convulsed with each muffled sob. On the table, the edge of a large knife danced in the candlelight.

A shadow fell across the boy as a woman appeared. Lifting the hem of her black dress, she shuffled her stooped body beside him, her long wild hair bouncing with every step. The orange glow flashed across the ridges of her wrinkled face.

The woman reached into her pocket. Lyndsay's hands shot to her mouth and she inhaled sharply as the woman withdrew a glowing green slug the length of her palm. She tilted the boy's head back and laid the wriggling creature across his forehead.

The boy's whimpers grew louder and he shook his head. His left eye closed as the slug slithered its thick green body over his eyelid and down his cheek. The woman clasped a hand on his shoulder, restraining him with a strength that belied her age.

Lyndsay's body shook, every rapid breath cutting the back of her dry throat.

What is...

The boy's nostril flared and pulsed, his cry becoming a choked wheeze as the slug squirmed its way inside his nose. The old woman released his shoulders and the boy's head flopped forwards, his body silent and still.

She's killed him.

The woman grabbed the knife from the table and cut the boy's bonds, her wrinkles spreading into a wicked grin. She wiped the sleeve of her dress across his eyelid, removing a glob of slime that had gathered there.

With a sudden jerk, the boy sat straight.

The woman stepped back as the boy opened his eyes, a faint green glow within their depths. A serrated cackle broke the silence as she clapped and hopped from one foot to the other.

I've got to get away from here.

Before Lyndsay could move, a hungry howl pierced the night.

Oh God. Buddy.

Her cold fingers fumbled with her zip. As it opened, a dull thud hit the stone path and clattered away from her.

A second howl rang out, louder this time, an urgency to its hunger.

Lyndsay caught movement in the corner of her eye and peered back through the window. The boy now stood. Both he and the old woman were staring straight at her.

Oh no.

Lyndsay jumped to her feet and covered her eyes as the security light bathed her in its harsh brilliance. One arm raised across her brow, she sprinted towards Cheriee.

"Run," she screamed as she leapt the fence.

"What's going on?" said Cheriee, suspicion in her eyes as they darted between Lyndsay and the house. "I'm not falling for your tricks, you know I don't believe in-"

"It's the boy," said Lyndsay, grabbing Cheriee's arm and dragging her away from the fence. "She's got him."

"The missing boy?" said Cheriee, her eyes wide now as she stumbled backwards. "Who's got him?"

A thunderous slam caused them both to shriek as the front door to the house flew open. An old woman bounded from the opening and raced across the grass with surprising speed.

"Her," shouted Lyndsay as she released Cheriee's arm.

They spun on their heels and sprinted towards the narrow entrance to lovers' lane. Plunged into darkness, the wind whipped at their hair as they ran down the lane as fast as they dared.

The pounding behind them grew louder.

They burst out the end of lovers' lane and sped past the old boating shed, heading towards the lights of the town centre.

Hissing breaths and heavy footsteps were right behind them.

"The river," shouted Lyndsay, cutting to her right. Cold shock washed over her as she splashed into the water.

"Help," shouted Cheriee.

Lyndsay turned to see her friend had fallen on the wet pebbles. The old woman gripped her ankle and was dragging her from the river.

Lyndsay staggered to reach Cheriee's outstretched arm but was suddenly plummeting, her feet betraying her on the slippery rocks.

Pain ripped through the back of her head and her vision sunk into a dizzying spin. She was vaguely aware that the chill of the water had coated her body, but she couldn't gather the thoughts required to raise her heavy limbs.

Closing her eyes, the screams faded as everything turned to black.

*

Lyndsay opened her eyes to see Cheriee sitting beside her in the field next to lovers' lane.

This... can't...

"Welcome back," said Cheriee, swigging from her

bottle of alcohol as she glanced down at her friend and then gazed across the field. "Too much of this peachy goodness?"

How did I…

Lyndsay shivered as she sat up, her drenched clothing clinging to her body. Brow creasing, she reached a hand to the back of her head and winced as she found the source of her headache. Nausea rose as her stomach twisted itself in knots.

Somethings off…

"Wh- what h- happened?" said Lyndsay, her teeth chattering. "W- where is she?"

"Who?" asked Cheriee, resting the bottle on her lap as she tilted her head to look at the moon, visible now the clouds had gone.

"Th- the old w- woman," said Lyndsay, her body shaking.

"What woman?" asked Cheriee with a giggle. "You drank too much and fell asleep on the wet grass."

Lyndsay's eyes narrowed.

What's going on?

She forced herself up onto quaking legs and crossed her arms, her damp face flinching at every bite of the wind.

Something's not quite… right…

Across the field, the moonlight picked out features of the silent house. The front door was closed and the living room window was dark.

She reached into her pocket to check if Buddy had got wet. Her heart skipped as she discovered he wasn't there.

Because I dropped him.

She turned to find Cheriee was also now standing and looking straight at her. She had one hand behind her back and a lopsided smile on her face.

That's when she realised what was causing the hair on her neck to stand on end. It wasn't the cold breeze on her wet skin or the throbbing at the back of her skull. It wasn't the missing pet that she knew still lay on a stone path outside the darkened house. It wasn't even the realisation that nobody knew she was here.

It was the faint green glow emanating from her friend's eyes.

Her jaw dropped as Cheriee bared her teeth in a manic grin.

"I believe now," said Cheriee, drawing her hand from behind her back to reveal a shimmering green slug, its pulsating body pinched between her finger and thumb. "Let me show you what Tam was running from."

7: CALL OF THE NUCKELAVEE

She gasped as her foot slipped at the top of the dune. Arms flailing, she tumbled over the high ridge and down the steep sandy embankment. Coarse grass and broken shells scratched at her palms and face as she slid to a halt at the bottom.

Need to be more careful.

Drawing deep gulps of air, she spat a glob of salty grit onto the sand and pushed herself to her knees. The soft pale sand, so beautiful from a distance, betrayed those who wandered too close to its edge. She knew this, but she didn't have a choice. The sea called to her, the promise of dark revelations on its lips. Confessing its misdeeds.

Scowling from the effort, she stood and brushed the sand from her thick coat and fleece-lined leggings.

Let's do this.

Tall and athletic, she strode across the beach with the assertive gait of an executioner. Her sturdy walking boots leaving heavy indents in the wet sand.

I'm Fiona Gunn. Daughter of the murdered Alistair

Gunn. And I'm coming for answers.

Under an angry sky, she followed the shoreline. The tide was out and her footsteps were the only blemishes on the lustrous surface. Steep hills and boggy marshes deterred all but the most determined walkers from this hidden cove.

The voice is stronger here. I'm close.

The wind whipped at her long black hair. She gripped her hood as the cold December rain beat down with greater force. The temperature had plummeted as the final rays of the sun disappeared over the horizon. Squinting through the stinging grit whipping her face, she scoured the darkened waves, searching for the source of the voice.

I know you're out there. I know what you did.

The turbulent waves chopped a blustery path to the shore. Their secrets hidden.

A year had passed since her father had died.

Alone. On a day like this, when nobody had any business being out in the wild.

She never got to say goodbye.

"Do you hear that?" he had said, before grabbing his coat and heading towards the door. Alfie, our golden Labrador, had followed him to the car. That was the last time she had seen either of them alive. Her father's body had washed up on the beach, drowned. Alfie was never found.

She had put it down to the drink.

Too many whiskies sunk since mum had died. Two parents lost. Both to the sea.

They had lived on a farm in Orkney, near the shore. Dad had described it as a run of bad luck. The wilted crops and spoiled grain, cows too sick to stand. Debts stacked up and relationships broke down. Mother, saddened by the loss of all she had worked for, took her own life by walking into the sea.

Or so we had thought.

All parents keep secrets from their children, but this was different. Grief had changed her father. He had become obsessed with walking the beach for hours. Angry outbursts cursing the world, followed by tearful prayers to the Mither o' the Sea, pleading for her to return what she had taken.

Our mother was gone, but something had heard him.

During restless sleep, he had cried out about the demon of the sea. When pressed about it he claimed he couldn't remember, but his eyes told a different story. They held an emotion she had never witnessed in her father. Fear.

Something had answered his prayers.

Something evil.

He spoke of hearing my mother's voice, calling to him, asking him to join her. It promised him things, though what he did not say. But she could guess.

Because it's his voice now whispering those promises. Calling to me.

She had inherited his delusions. The cold chill of hearing the voice of her dead father carried on the wind. Begging her to join him, promising to be a family again.

She stopped as the first waves broke over her boots. The deep rumble of the sea thundered through her head, its furthest reaches now lost to the dark of night.

I'm coming for you.

After her father had died, she had sold what was left of the farm and moved to the mainland. Settling in Castletown, she thought she had left the misery behind.

But then his voice had spoken to her. Whispers at first, calling her to the shore.

The thing that had killed her father had followed her

here.

It wants me.

Like her father, she had turned to the drink, trying to drown out its constant demand. She cried and screamed and shouted at the wind. At night she tossed and turned, waking with sheets soaked through. The mirror reflected the same thing she had seen in her father's eyes.

Fear.

She couldn't reveal that she was hearing voices. Instead, searching for answers, she had turned to the old ways for help. She devoured books of myths and legends of the sea, left offerings by the shore to appease the ancient Gods, trying to rid herself of her father's voice. None had worked, he called out stronger than ever.

Begging to see his daughter.

Desperate, she crept one night into the ruins of St Trothan's church. Gently dipping her bare foot into the small hollow of the selkie's grave, she had wished for the voice to be gone. Neither the magic of the selkie nor the Mither o' the Sea had listened, but something had heard her. Cruel laughter on the wind had echoed around the graveyard, chasing her away.

That's when she knew it wasn't her father.

It's something older. Darker. Something that feasts on the misery of man.

She didn't know why it had cast its malicious gaze upon her family, but she was determined to get answers tonight.

Her eyes caught movement on the distant dunes.

A dog was racing across the beach towards the sea. Its golden coat shimmered in the low light of the rising moon.

Alfie.

The dog stopped and stared at her before tilting its

head back to release a mournful howl. It paced back and forth at the edge of the shoreline.

He wants me to follow.

The dog crisscrossed its circular path as she walked towards it.

Has the sea has returned him to me?

As she drew near, the dog surged into the crashing waves, rising and falling as it drifted away from shore.

She broke into a run, leaping waves until she splashed into the icy chill of the deeper water.

Where's he gone?

The dog had disappeared behind a large wave and not re-emerged. She waded through the raging sea until the water reached her chest, her breath coming in short frigid gasps. She thought she could see him, a dark shape in the water, just a bit further out.

She ducked her shoulders into the water and kicked off from the seabed. Her coat weighing her down as her arms struggled to propel her forwards, fighting against the swell of the rough waters.

Just a little further.

She kicked and swam until she lurked above the dark shape in the water. She tried to stand but found the water was too deep. She breathed through her nose as her mouth sank beneath the surface, her tired limbs fighting to keep her afloat.

"Alfie," she cried, struggling to raise her mouth and voice above the rush and roar of the waves.

Something brushed against her leg.

The darkness in the water was moving below her.

She reached down with a heavy arm, missing the shape as water crashed over her head, forcing her beneath the surface. She bobbed back up and gasped for air.

That's when she noticed it.

The voice is gone.

With a deep breath, she forced herself to reach down once more. Her fingertips brushed against something soft that moved to elude her grasp.

There was laughter now. The same cruel cackle that had driven from the selkie's grave.

"Where are you?" she shouted to the angry sea.

Something bumped into her, harder this time. She felt it wrap around her leg and pull her down, saltwater flooding into her mouth as she gasped before going under.

Panic coursed through her as she blindly thrashed and tore at the thing that gripped her leg. Her lungs burned and her heartbeat thumped in her head as it dragged her deeper.

Not like this.

Her fingers caught on a slimy band. She felt a snap and found herself released to kick and splutter to the surface once more. She coughed and spat and tried to swim back towards the shore. She could see it now, larger than before. A dark shape just below the surface, heading towards her.

It wants me.

Suddenly she was thrust backwards by a huge wave as the black shape broke the surface of the water. Her toes brushed against the seabed and she kicked and flapped until she could stand. The shape rose higher, the giant rippling waves of its emergence trying to beat her exhausted body back beneath the water. But she stood firm, trembling with cold and fear as she stared up at the monstrosity silhouetted by the light of the moon.

It stood three times the height of a man. A colossal horse's head with a single glaring red eye that pierced through the darkness. Upon its back was a man-shaped creature, though where horse ended and rider began she couldn't tell, their bodies fused in a sickening twist of melded sinew. Great clawed hands hung at the end of long arms that skimmed the surface of the water. One claw gripped the remains of what once had been a dog, now decaying and bloated by the sea.

She staggered back, her scream lost in the howl of the wind. She had seen this creature in the books of myths and legends. She recognised its face from half-recalled nightmares.

The nuckelavee.

The skinless creature paced towards her, the moonlight reflecting off bare muscle and bleached bone. The pungent smell of sulphur and decay emanated from the beast. With every step, its body pulsed in a disgusting mimicry of a foul tide.

She took another step back, the water now at her waist.

The rider's face split open to reveal two rows of long sharp teeth. A voice called to her. No longer her father's, but the sound of a thousand tortured souls crying out as one.

Come to me.

She dared another step back.

A deafening howl rang out as the creature reared up onto its hind legs, before slamming its hooves back down into the water. It moved towards her, faster now.

She stumbled as her foot caught on a rock.

The horse head snorted as the creature stalked a few steps closer. Its single red eye fixed on its prey.

"Why," she screamed, regaining her footing. "Why us?"

A familiar laugh cut across the gap between them.

With a gentle splash, the surface of the water broke to the left of the creature.

The rider turned its head, its mouth gaping with a threatening roar.

A small black head with large round eyes watched her as it bobbed on the water. With a low growl, it dived beneath the surface again, the moonlight dancing across its sleek skin.

A seal.

The horse-creature stopped, its human head darting back and forth across the water. It discarded the body of the dog as it plunged its claws in and out of the waves.

The seal burst out of the water again on the opposite side of the creature. Closer this time.

The horse turned and drove a cloven hoof at the seal, but it was already gone, its agility far outmatching the power of the lumbering beast.

The seal emerged in front of me. Its short urgent barks were human-like in their warning. Its wide eyes gleaming with deep intelligence. It was more than seal, she could see that now.

Her wish had been granted.

A selkie.

Renewed determination flooded her body.

She turned and ran towards the beach.

The creature released an anguished howl as hooves galloped through the water behind her.

As she hit the shore, the last of her energy left her body and she collapsed on the wet sand.

An angry shriek cut through the night, followed by a great splash.

Gasping, she looked out to sea.

The creature was gone.

She lay her exhausted head on the sand, her chest rising and falling with deep gulps of air as she listened to the waves. They were calmer now, their anger dissipated.

She had her answers.

He didn't leave me, he was taken.

She sat up and held her face in her hands. Her body shook with cold and painful sobs.

"Goodbye dad," she whispered before she stood and began the long climb back up the dunes.

The wind had died down. The voice was gone.

Today she had finally laid her father to rest.

Tomorrow she would lay flowers at the selkie's grave, dip her foot in the watery hollow, and pray that she never again heard the call of the nuckelavee.

8: BLACK DOG IN THE
DEVIL'S BOTHY

She knew that life came with edges, but of all the horrors she thought she would face on this mountain, she never imagined blisters to be the worst. Cursing, she limped beneath the wet branches of a stunted oak and dumped her rucksack on the sodden floor.

Small plastic plasters coiled loosely in her sock, sweated off and causing more pain than they were preventing. The rain had soaked through her thin coat and the midges were growing fat around her. She slumped to the ground and slapped the back of her neck as another joined the feast.

This was supposed to be relaxing.

A gentle hike in the Scottish Highlands. The beauty of the land chasing away the demon that resides in her mind. The black dog that lurks in the dark, stealing her sleep and whispering fears of things to come. A hound that spends its days digging through her memories, terrorising her with the long-dead skeletons it uncovers.

This combined assault had caused '*the incident*' at

work. Now lost and labelled, she fought a daily battle, while her therapist worked to banish the demon for good. On his recommendation, she had booked a guesthouse in Glencoe and planned to hike the west ridge of Beinn a' Chrulaiste.

Pamaljit the lawyer becomes Pam the explorer.

It will be good for your health, the website had said. It will be great for your mind, her therapist had affirmed. It will be fantastic for your waistline, her family had exclaimed, suggesting it might even help her find a man. Then she could get her job back. Perhaps even have a baby or three.

Stress. Stress. Stress.

The pressure had grown when her two younger sisters had got married, and now three children in the world called her aunty. Over the years her parent's hopeful questions had become disapproving glares and condemnation. Even Monwara, her best friend, had stopped defending her choices.

Your eggs are drying up. Stop eating junk. Get out more.

Except now that she was out, she desperately wanted to be back inside. The hike had been a failure from the start. Her new trainers rubbed her skin raw almost immediately and a storm cloud moved in before she had reached the hour mark.

But it looked so beautiful this morning.

Confident the trees would provide shelter from the rain, she had left the grassy path that trailed up the mountain and walked into the forest. Shortly after, the weight of her rucksack began dragging her down, pulling at muscles she wasn't aware she had. Now she didn't know how many hours had passed, but she didn't feel relaxed.

Lost in her thoughts, she had been dimly aware of the forest changing around her. The wide path and thin lines had become dense rows erupting from the matted undergrowth. Bursts of birdsong had been replaced with ominous creaking and hammering rain. Sprawling branches had blocked her route, whipping her as she pushed her way past.

Soaked through to her skin, every step had become more painful than the last.

Time to give up and go back.

Her legs and back ached as she stood and stretched. She heaved her rucksack onto her shoulders and stared up as the rain battered the trees, releasing the earthy smells of the forest. She breathed deeply, held it a moment, and then let it out in a long sigh. Twigs cracked and leaves squelched underfoot as she set off on what she believed to be a shortcut back to a more civilised path.

Her stride soon became a frustrated hobble.

How is anybody supposed to find their way around here, it all looks the same.

As she rounded a pair of broad pines, she saw the forest thinning ahead, revealing a glade bathed in a faint fog that covered the ground.

Wait, what's that?

Nestled within the fog, she spied a small cabin. Its grey stone walls and moss-covered roof jarred against the landscape. Its squared angles sitting unnaturally amidst the wild tumble of the organic domain. With no windows in sight, its wind-scoured door was closed, the pathway choked with brambles.

A bothy.

She quickened her pace and staggered into the glade, hoping to soon be out the rain. She had read about bothies in the brochure, public cabins in remote locations across the Scottish mountains.

And I've found one just when I need it.

Ignoring the sting of the brambles, she crossed the glade until she stood in a flat grassy area before the door. The bare wood contained specks of red paint within its deepest groves, and a round brass handle turned green by years of exposure. Nailed across the door was a small plank of wood that had a single word burned into its centre.

Diabhal. Probably the name of a hill or something.

The slanted roof drove the rainwater off its side. It gushed in running waves that doused the nearby undergrowth in a torrent of moss-infused splatters.

At least it'll be dry inside.

The handle resisted her first attempt, before turning with a faint click. She leaned her weary body against the door and pushed. It opened with a heavy creak.

She coughed as dust hit her lungs, the musty smell of old wood imbued with the heady scents of the forest. The light from the door revealed a small windowless room, its bare stone walls and rough wooden floor untouched by the elements.

Empty. That's good.

She stepped inside the door, closing it just enough to keep the worst of the rain out. Trudging over to the corner furthest from the opening, she dropped her rucksack to the floor. She peeled off her sodden coat and slung it next to the rucksack. Her trainers went next, kicked to the wall, closely followed by her soaking wet socks.

Standing barefoot, she winced as her wiggling toes discovered new blisters. With a sigh, she sat in the corner, legs outstretched and back resting against the sturdy stone wall as she examined the room.

Good, no spiders.

She reached over and dug her phone out of her rucksack. The screen was damp and had a little red cross next to the signal, but it still glowed with a half-full battery. It told her she had been walking for four and a half hours, the furthest she ever remembered walking in her life.

Well, at least that's something.

The dull ache in her legs and back had spread to every part of her body, middle-age and a sedentary lifestyle catching up with her. She had intended to be better prepared for the hike, but somehow never found the motivation to begin.

Too tired all the time.

The wind whipped through the branches outside. The rain thumped against the roof, but she now found its irregular beat soothing. She lay her head back against the wall and closed her eyes, letting the hypnotic rhythm of the rain calm her mind as she waited for the storm to pass.

"Hello," said a voice.

Pain shot through her limbs as she jolted awake, her wide eyes scanning the empty room.

Inhaling rapidly, she watched as an unseen hand began to creak the door closed.

Her heart plummeted as the wind roared through the smallest of gaps before the door clicked shut and she was plunged into darkness.

Her hearing sprang alive, her pulse thundering in her head. She scraped her back against the wall as she scrambled to her feet.

"Who- who's there?" she stuttered.

"It's only me Pam," said the voice.

"How do you… who are you?"

"You know who I am," said the voice. "Everybody who finds their way here recognises me."

I must be hallucinating. I've finally lost my mind.

"Not yet," said the voice.

"Wha… are you in my head?"

"Oh I'm always around," said the voice. "Watching… waiting."

A wave of heat washed over her face as she darted across the room. Her palms slapped and rubbed against the wall, blindly searching for the door.

She could only feel the bare stone.

Where is it?

She stepped sideways, running her hand the full length of the wall.

The door was gone.

Impossible. How?

A mocking laugh echoed around the pitch-black room. She spun on her heels. Waves of heat rose from the stone against her back and the wood warmed beneath her soles.

"Once you're in the dark place, it's not so easy to get out," said the voice.

"What do you want?" said Pam, a dry cough scratching her throat. The hiss of water being seared from wet clothing was accompanied by the stench of damp odours steamed from sweaty fabrics. Her jumper became unbearably hot.

She reached out a trembling hand and touched the wall, snapping it back as her fingertips pressed against the scalding stone. Her vision swam as she pulled her jumper over her head, dropped it to the floor and leapt onto it to relieve her burning feet.

"What do you want?" she screamed to the darkness.

"I want to keep you here," said the voice. "But being

human, the rules dictate that you have a choice."

Pam coughed again, the vapours from her steaming clothes itching and clogging her throat.

Need a light. My phone.

She stepped towards her rucksack but shrunk back from the scorching heat of the wooden floor. Tearing off her t-shirt, she crouched to feel for the edge of her jumper. She slung the t-shirt beyond this, where it sizzled and spat like a freshly cracked egg. She stepped onto the t-shirt and reached into the darkness.

Not far enough.

Her thumbs hesitated on the waistband of her tracksuit bottoms before she ripped them off and flicked them out in front of her. She heard them smack against the wall. Laying them next to her t-shirt, she shuffled along them until the heat from the stone wall was directly in front of her.

She stooped and groped where she had left her rucksack. Her heart sank as she grasped only air, earning scalded knuckles as they brushed against the blistering stone.

Gone too.

She stood and wiped the back of her forearm across her furrowed brow. Sweat beads trickled down her back as the sweltering heat blazed against her bare skin.

"It seems like your choice is made," said the voice.

"What choice?" she croaked.

"Give yourself over to me and stay here in my dark place," purred the voice. "It's warm and I can shelter you from the storm."

Pam stepped back onto her t-shirt and wiped her palms over her face.

It's not a choice when there's only one option.

The voice snarled. "Or you can keep up this pathetic struggle and face your fears."

Pam shivered, despite the heat. Her shoulders sagged and she lowered herself onto her makeshift rug. She tucked her knees to her chest, cradled them with her arms and rested her throbbing forehead against them.

Wake up. Please wake up. I don't want to die like this.

"Are you sure? Because you chose to live like this." said the voice. "Hidden away from the world in your dark place. Losing sight of the things that were important to you."

"I didn't have a choice," she whispered.

I can't control my feelings.

"Then they control you," said the triumphant voice. "They make the choice for you."

Pam nodded to the dark. She understood that her actions were often dictated by her emotions, something her therapist was working to overcome.

Always trying to give me hope. My defences come up and my energy goes down. Too exhausted to keep up appearances, it's easier to push people away.

"So here you'll stay," said the voice. "Alone."

Pam shook her head.

If I stay here I'll die.

She released her knees and stood up.

And as difficult as each battle may be, I'm not ready to lose this war.

"I want to leave," said Pam.

"Very well," said the voice. "Then you must answer my question correctly."

A test.

"Imagine you are in a dark room," said the voice. "How do you get out?"

Pam tilted her head. "That's the question?"

"Yes," said the voice. "Are you feeling the heat? You had better hurry with your answer."

"But I am in a dark room," said Pam. "And there's no way out?"

Cruel laughter boomed against the walls, causing Pam to cower and cover her ears.

Ok, think Pam.

The fetid stench of burning cloth wafted from the floor. Her brown skin prickled, as she choked on fiery air.

Think. You're here. Imagine you are in a dark room. How do you get out? A door? A window?

She didn't have either of those.

"I don't know the answer," said Pam, her dry eyes stinging as she fell to her knees. "Please just let me out?"

"I'm afraid I can't do that," growled the voice. "You chose to come here."

Pam tried to scream, but her burning throat cut her off in a hacking cough. Rivulets of sweat rolled across her body as the last of her energy withered away.

She could hear it breathing now, the impatient panting of a hungry animal.

"When the black clouds descended, you ignored the warning signs," said the voice. "You retreated inside to hide from the storm. And I was here for you."

"I- I didn't understand the sign," whispered Pam, her hands pressed over her mouth and nose.

"No, of course you didn't," taunted the voice. "The one that stands before the door is always the last to heed the signs."

Retching from the bitter tang of veiled smoke, she fumbled for the wall, her nails scraping against the searing stone.

This can't be real. Think Pam.

"You ran away and hid like you always do," said the voice, closer now.

The room filled with the harsh scraping of a dog's claws as it walked across the wooden floor.

"You're weak Pam," snarled the voice. "Not clever enough to save yourself. Not brave enough."

Oh God, I'm imagining this. I must be… hold on, that's it. Imagine you are in a dark room. How do you get out? You stop imagining it.

"Stop imagining it," shouted Pam to the darkness, her voice hoarse. "That's my answer."

The voice barked a vicious laugh. "Too late."

Pam turned to face the wall where she knew the door should be.

If I'm imagining this darkness, I can imagine something else.

She jumped to her feet and kicked the wall with her bare heel. A dog howled as a tiny sliver of light appeared in the bricks. She kicked again, ignoring the smell and agony of her burning flesh. More cracks appeared, spreading now, as the light grew.

"Stop that," growled the voice. She screamed as sharp teeth sunk into her arm, pulling her back into the dark depths of the room. Fighting and stumbling, she kicked out one final time.

The wall collapsed.

She scrunched her eyes and turned her head as bright light burst into the room.

The dog released its grip on her arm, the momentum propelling her through the blinding breach. She threw her hands out to break her fall, her body embracing a soft and soothing cold.

Turning, she saw that she had tumbled through the bothy door and now lay in the wet grass. Looking around, she noticed the forest was glistening, the warm sun glinting off raindrops that had settled on the blossoming flora.

The storm has passed.

She stood and peered back through the door. She could see her clothes strewn across the wooden floor, her rucksack leaning against the wall next to her discarded shoes. She wrapped her arms around herself and smiled. The trees maintained their mute observance as she realised there were no burns on her hands or teeth marks on her arm.

I made it.

Tears streamed freely down her cheeks as she turned towards the sun, letting its warmth caress her skin.

"I made it," she yelled, extending her arms in the air. "I beat you."

Because I understand you now.

She wiped her cheeks and breathed in the fresh forest air.

When the black clouds roll in, we ignore the warning signs and seek shelter within our minds. We slam the door shut.

She now knew that she had been placing herself in that room for many years, feeding the black dog that lives there. Every fear she bowed down to, and each regret she couldn't let go, gave power to that dark place.

Then suddenly we are alone, fighting a battle that others cannot see. That we don't let them see, our deepest wounds hidden from our closest allies.

She dug her toes into the grass as she picked her way past the brambles towards the ancient pines. Pools of water gathered and trickled over her feet with every step.

I always ignored the warning signs. The tiredness. The irritability. Pushing friends and family away.

She grabbed a handful of leaves, lifting them to her nose and inhaling their crisp scent, before letting them fall back to the ground.

But there's always a glimmer of light in the dark, waiting to be discovered.

She gazed up through the thick canopy, marvelling at the beams of sunlight fighting their way through the branches to alight upon the forest floor. Its muted glow comforting as it softly nourished the verdant glade.

We have to face that black dog and save ourselves. Stop trapping ourselves in that dark place with fears of the future and pains of the past. Focus on the light and imagine a way out.

She tilted her head back and closed her eyes.

We must choose to be kind to ourselves. Because even though we are only human, we always have a choice.

9: LAST TRAIN SOUTH

Kerry's hands burned as she struggled to lift the suitcase, the skin rubbed raw from a night spent erasing her past. Despite her best efforts, she couldn't quite raise it over the step and onto the train.

A shadow appeared at the side of her vision.

"Do you need a hand with that?" asked a gentleman wearing a conductor's uniform, his breath visible in the cold November air.

Kerry winced as her back stiffened and her hands gripped the suitcase handle.

Just breathe, it'll be fine.

She stared at the badge on the man's chest, unable to lift her head to meet his gaze.

He doesn't know. Don't panic.

Her heart hammered as she gave a quick nod, before shoving her bloodied palms into the pockets of her long thick coat. She watched as the conductor strained to lift the suitcase, eventually scraping it over the lip of the step.

"Wow, you don't travel light," he said, catching his

breath.

Kerry forced a thin smile of thanks and stepped onto the train. Peering through the carriage door to her right she spotted a middle-aged couple sitting at a table. The woman read a book while the man stretched and settled back in his seat, ready to doze away the journey. As she watched, a younger man boarded the train at the end of the carriage. Headphones in, he didn't even glance up as he swung his backpack onto a vacant seat and sat beside it.

Too many witnesses.

She turned and looked through the other carriage door. It was empty.

Perfect.

The door slid open to greet her with a whiff of body odour and stale crisps. She knew the train had already made this journey once today, a four and a half hour crawl along the coastline from Wick to Inverness.

The last train south.

Wheeling the heavy suitcase inside, she realised it was too large to fit inside the luggage bay. Positioning it in the centre of the aisle behind the door, she chose a table seat facing it and sat down.

Stay calm. You can do this.

She had made it. After a full night of cleaning and scrubbing, hiding and destroying, she had sorted her affairs and made her way to the station. The kids were at their grandparents. Hastily arranged, but decisions had to be made.

And final decisions had definitely been made. Motivated by the strength of conviction that only decisions made late at night can hold.

A sudden movement.

Kerry slid down in her seat and held her breath as a

woman entered the train. She peered through the carriage door at the suitcase blocking the way. Kerry tucked her chin, watching the woman from the corner of her vision. With a disapproving glare, the woman turned and entered the other carriage.

"Thank you," Kerry whispered, the words released in a long sigh as she straightened her back. She gently swept her fingers over her brow, smoothing down her freshly-dyed brown hair. Cut short this morning into a bob, it framed her oval face in a way that he would never have approved of. She had yearned to drift to sleep as the stylist massaged her scalp, the long sleepless night threatening to catch up with her. It was the fear of what happens next that kept her awake.

She cupped her damaged hands over large brown eyes that had cried far too many tears, her fingertips feeling their way along the creases in her brow.

Nearly forty and my frown lines cut deeper than any others.

She ran her tongue over the grooves she had bitten into her thin lips. Parting her fingers, she stared at the suitcase. She had purchased it new today, in a hurry, the largest one she could find. It bulged with its awkwardly packed contents, chopped and sealed; she prayed it would hold them for just a few more hours.

So close now.

She let her hands fall to her lap and grimaced as she instinctively wrung them. Annoyed with herself, she trapped them between her thighs. She had found herself doing that a lot more since this had all started.

Since my world had crumbled.

The first few days had been terrible. Their home had become a courtroom, her heart the judge ready to wield the hammer. The jury had filed in one or two at a time; friends and family delivering their verdict on a man they all believed was guilty.

And he was.

Unable to bear the pain alone, she had called on a key witness, her best friend. Bursting through her front door in tears, it had all poured out. The betrayal, the sleepless nights, the thoughts of revenge. Through intense sobs she had told the full story, hollowing herself out.

She sighed. That had been weeks ago now. She had confided in one other person since then. Pacts of friendship had been sealed.

And we had formed the plan.

The shrill peep of the conductor's whistle brought her thoughts to order. As the train doors sounded their warning alarm, she glanced once more at the evidence blocking the aisle.

Closing her eyes, she rocked gently with the rumble of the train as it began its journey. She had memorised the route.

Rest until we reach Muir of Ord. Then prepare myself for the stop at Beauly.

The train had warmed and she tugged at her collar and opened the top button of her coat. She became aware her knee was rapidly bouncing and made a conscious effort to restrain it.

Reaching into her pocket, she pulled out a bar of chocolate. A shiver of excitement tingled through her body, like a prisoner's giddy high on their first day of release. He had never let her eat chocolate. He made it clear that she had to stay thin, and because she didn't want to lose him, she was guilty of losing herself.

Foolish.

She tore the wrapper open and took a large bite, enjoying the way it melted on her tongue. Tears formed as she thought of all the time she had wasted trying to make him happy, always falling short.

It was never enough. I was never enough.

She took another bite. She knew breakups were more difficult now she was older. They were messier. When you are young and carefree there's always another boy to distract you. You recover quickly, your whole life still ahead of you, the possibilities endless.

But I had ignored all the red flags.

It was these regrets which had caused sleepless nights these past few weeks.

Setbacks affect you more. Wounds cut deeper.

We lose a soul mate, a friend and a life together. Our children lose the security and stability of happy parents. The family home becomes a battleground, social media a spiteful competition to see who can fake the finest life. Truth is lost amidst petty lies.

But still, we persevere. Make the best of it.

Recovery begins by putting our own happiness first. We all make mistakes, but life goes on. Our circle shrinks, but true friends reveal themselves. Our allies and accomplices.

Plans are made and ruthlessly executed. The mess can be scrubbed away.

A hard bump pulled her from her thoughts. Driving rain beat against the window, streaking across the glass. Through the gloom, the Highland scenery rolled by. She scratched the back of her hand. They were thinner now, a combination of her growing confidence in the gym and her lack of appetite. Yawning, she raised her legs to stretch the exhaustion from her body.

Suddenly, he was there.

Though she knew he couldn't possibly be.

He sat opposite her, staring out the window, nonchalantly watching the world go by.

W-What…

Her eyes darted between him and the suitcase. His skin unblemished, his body whole. The accused had entered the room.

She screwed her eyes shut.

When she opened them again he turned to look at her, his eyes alive, challenging her conviction.

A cold shiver of guilt trickled down her spine as she placed the remainder of the chocolate bar onto the table.

Unblinking, he met her terrified gaze.

"H- How?" she croaked, her voice breaking. She folded her arms to stop her hands from trembling.

He looked at the suitcase and shook his head.

She knew this wasn't real. Her broken mind was cross-examining events.

Like the voices that had decided his fate.

Two in the morning.

"Has the jury reached a decision?"

"We have, your honour."

"How do you find the accused on the charge of ruining my life?"

Her mind had become clear that night. Thoughts focused and collaborators recruited, the plan had formed. Even now, her two closest friends waited to play their part. There were no objections.

"Guilty, your honour."

He was the one responsible, not me, though we often blame ourselves. We think we deserve the things that happen to us. The way somebody loves us, though, is often a reflection of the way we love ourselves. If we can even call it love at all.

"The accused has shown no remorse."

Our actions have taught them how to treat us. How we speak about ourselves and allow ourselves to be treated. If we don't respect ourselves, we show them that they don't need to either.

But we can also show them that there are consequences. That every crime has a punishment.

She set her jaw, unfolded her arms and picked up the bar of chocolate. Taking a large bite, she looked him straight in the eye, chewing slowly before taking another.

"Will the accused please rise?"

Sometimes we have to be undervalued before we realise our worth.

Undervalued and underestimated.

"You have been found guilty. I hereby sentence you to…"

She screwed her eyes shut and counted to ten before opening them again.

The sentence had been passed.

He was gone.

She wiped at a trickle of chocolatey drool and lifted her heavy head. A dull pain throbbed in her neck and her back clicked as she straightened her posture. The conductor announced that the next station was Beauly.

What? Did I fall asleep?

She glanced at the suitcase.

It was nearly time.

She jumped out of her seat and hit the open button on the carriage door. Dragging the suitcase, she waited by the outer door. Her heart raced and between rapid breaths she prayed the others hadn't backed out.

I can do this.

As the train slowed, she looked past her harried reflection. Through the early evening darkness, she could make out hedges and fences rolling by, which abruptly gave way to platform.

The train came to a stop opposite a small sheltered area. A young couple stepped forward, holding hands as they waited for the door to open. A third figure hung back beneath the sheltered roof, the hood of a large black coat hiding their face in shadow.

She jolted as the door alarm sounded. A cold breeze slapped across her face as the doors slid open and she stepped aside so the couple could climb aboard. They entered the carriage she had just vacated.

Doesn't matter.

The hooded figure stepped into the rain and reached out a gloved hand.

The door alarm rang out again, signalling its imminent closure.

Kerry wheeled the suitcase to the top of the step, set her feet and then pushed with both hands. The suitcase tumbled down the step and onto the platform, just as the doors slid shut.

The train rocked as it carried on its journey.

Pressing her face against the window, she could see the figure disappearing from view. Their familiar gait dragging the suitcase behind them.

It's over.

She leaned her back against the door and flicked her eyes between the carriages. Nobody stirred. The middle-aged couple were both asleep. The young man still sat with his headphones in, scrolling through his phone. The disapproving woman was gone, having likely departed at an earlier stop. The young couple who had just boarded were removing wet coats. They hadn't noticed a thing.

No witnesses.

She had been prepared to run. To fight if she must. But nobody came for her. There were no sirens. No shouting or accusing fingers pointed her way. She knew in seventeen minutes she could step from the train and begin her new life. The plan had worked.

I have the best friends.

She turned to look at her reflection in the window. She let her jaw drop open and widened her eyes, before breaking into a smile.

Will need to work on my shocked face.

The train arrived at the station and she landed on the platform with a spring in her step. He was finally gone. Tonight, a hundred miles away, a mysterious fire would remove all evidence of her past life.

A fresh start.

I really do have the best friends.

She would pick her kids up and hold them tight and they would get through this as a family. Tonight though, she had one last thing to do.

Establish an alibi.

Because sometimes you just have to drop your baggage off and get on with life.

10: STOLEN PEACE

You could read as much or as little as you cared. That was the appeal of wild camping. Read when light, sleep when dark, the chaos of the world replaced by the simplest of pleasures. Of course, you had to gather wood for the fire and eat and drink. Answer the call of nature and hide from trained killers stalking you through the woods, but these were temporary distractions from an otherwise peaceful day lost within the pages of a splendid book.

For a burnt-out nuclear biologist on an unexpected break, it was the perfect way to spend his final days. He leaned his back against the tree and stretched his legs in the warm sun. He smiled as the gentle breeze caressed his face, fresh winds blowing across Loch Garve. The rocks and rigours of his escape successfully navigated, it was time to unwind.

It was the silence he truly appreciated. The miles of beauty that lay untouched by human endeavour.

And now I don't have to share it.

He dug his wedding ring out of his pocket. Little more

than a tie to a forgotten life, he drew his arm back and launched it towards the water. It disappeared into the depths with a delicate plop, its ripples the final remnants of something that had once meant so much.

He knew they would look for him, of course.

Probably searching for me now, if they have discovered it's missing.

He opened his book and attempted to read, but the ring had forced his thoughts back to the betrayal.

Had she ever loved me? When had they turned her?

Years of his life wasted on one who plotted to steal his secrets. Sweet whispers meant to guide his hand against his better judgement. Once he had discovered how they intended to use his serum, he had no choice but to flee to the safety of the woods.

He knew he would have to put the book away soon. Say goodbye to the much-loved characters he had befriended within its pages. Only ever able to visit its locales within his imagination.

A twig snapped behind him.

Reality strikes again.

With a sigh, he rose to his feet and drew the long hunting knife at his waist.

One way or another, the trip was over.

Both an ending and a beginning about to play out, but for who was not yet written.

He could see him now, a hunter in military uniform, lurking behind a tall pine tree.

"Dr Mackay," said the rough voice. "We don't want to hurt you. We just need it back."

"You don't understand," he said. "You can't control it."

"Then come back with me, help us understand."

"It's too late for that. The world stands on a precipice. I

won't be the one to tip us over the edge."

The bullet struck his chest and he fell to the floor, his knife flung into the undergrowth.

Struggling for breath, he reached into his pocket and withdrew a small vial. Popping the stopper, he strained to lift his neck and swallow the glowing blue liquid.

I only wanted some peace to read.

A familiar story, he thought, as his veins flooded with an angry power. To save his life, he had become a monster. The skin healed rapidly over his wound, flesh and sinew knitting itself together, stronger than before.

He rose to his feet and bellowed a challenge to the woods, his cry signalling the dawn of a new chapter of human history.

THE STORY BEHIND THE STORIES

I have included this section to provide a little insight into the childhood events and life experiences that inspired me to write each of these short stories.

Disclaimer: If any kids are reading this – don't do any of the things mentioned in this section of the book.

The Road Trip

This story was inspired by a ghost story a fellow author told one night when we were plotting story ideas. It stuck in my head because I have been on a lot of road trips through the Highlands, staying in many different guesthouses along the way.

In a few of these, I have found random items left behind by previous guests and wondered what the story was. Why were these items left here, even after the room had been tidied by the owner? Had they left in a hurry? Or had they even left at all? I'm sure I read a story somewhere about people living in the walls? Or maybe I just stayed in some dodgy places – I assumed the red lamp was for aesthetic.

During the road trips, I passed many small, overgrown roads which seemingly disappear off up a mountain. You only have to drive out to the Grey Cairns of Camster to get a sense of the isolation and an off-the-beaten-track experience. I imagined what it would be like to stay at one of the beautiful-but-ruined houses I passed on the way. Of course, being me, I then turned it supernatural.

I used to time my road trips with my birthday week, so I could spend it with family and childhood friends in Scotland, as well as visit the Edinburgh Christmas Markets. However, having a birthday at the end of November meant that we were often driving in difficult conditions.

On one particular journey, we were doing the road trip in my friend's rear-wheel drive BMW. It was a great car and easy journey until we entered a snowstorm. We couldn't even see the end of the bonnet. We were sliding into the oncoming lane, but were not in a good place to stop. So we persevered, very slowly. Eventually, we pulled up behind a Range Rover. It was being slowed by a very small car in front of it.

Between the three of us, we got the Range Rover to take the lead, and then we followed in the tracks it was making in the snow. Me being my usual self and laughing in the face of death – as the snowstorm began, I made a short video of it on my phone and posted it on social media with the tagline 'If you don't hear from us again, you know why'.

However, the journey then took us absolutely ages as we crawled along – and we lost mobile phone signal. Which caused a few people to get a bit upset over our whereabouts, including my road trip buddy's girlfriend. Long story short – we survived, but their relationship didn't!

Going over Berriedale Braes when there is ice on the road is one of my worst driving experiences. One very early morning I witnessed a car spinning out in front of me at the top of the hill. Fortunately, the driver regained control without serious incident. As a whole, this stretch of road still remains one of my favourite drives though and I knew I wanted to create tension in my story by starting it at this stage of the road trip.

In real-life, this route forms part of the stunning North Coast 500 driving route. A road trip that everybody should take at least once in their lives. I might be a bit biased when I say that you should plan extra days exploring Caithness.

I knew I wanted to open this entire collection with a traditional style ghost story, overtly located in the Highlands, with a bit of mystery and twist at the end. I wanted Maggie Munro to speak a mixture of Gaelic and an older Scots dialect, in order to enhance the unease of the characters as they ventured into the unknown, far away from what they had expected.

Secrets of the River

This was actually the first of the stories that I wrote for this collection. It was also my first foray into the mystery thriller genre. It reads a lot more literary and descriptively poetic than the other stories, as I felt it helped the pacing of the plot.

I spent a lot of time up Wick River during my childhood and always had a fascination for what may be hidden in the water. Some of the story is also based on real-life historical events. I liked the idea that something big, important and world-changing could be going on in a little café in the Highlands. With all of us oblivious to it.

Wick has some lovely cafés, with very friendly people that work in them. Which, for me, made the ominous and deadly elements of the story all that more compelling, as it's so different from everyday life. The rain though, that's sometimes realistic, though not as often as you might think.

The picture of the watercolour boats bobbing in the harbour was obviously inspired by Wick Harbour, another place I have spent a lot of time – both as an adult and while skipping school.

Before moving back to Scotland, I lived in Chipping Norton. My daughter went to St Mary's Primary School, which is associated with St Mary's Church in the town itself. During the Buckinghamshire and Oxfordshire Rising of 1549, a soldier called William Grey, the 13th Baron Grey de Wilton, lead a group of mercenary soldiers to put down the rebellion.

The uprising had been triggered by the introduction of the new English Prayer Book under King Edward VI. A vicar local to Chipping Norton was one of the leaders of the unrest. He was eventually arrested and hung in chains from the tower of St Mary's Church until he died.

There's a game that the children of Chipping Norton used to play which involved running around the graveyard outside the church three times at night. This would then apparently allow you to see a man hanging from the top of the church tower.

What's creepy is that none of these children were aware of the history of the church. Yet a game had somehow been created where they saw an apparition of a very specific real-life event that had occurred in that exact spot.

All ghost stories have to start somewhere. It makes you wonder though who invented the game and what they saw that made them create it.

On a lighter note, there's also a café in Chipping Norton whose walls are covered with old theatre posters, some of which are displaying local productions from Chipping Norton Theatre.

Another beautiful café there displays artwork from the local area, venerating life in the Cotswolds. Having lunch there one day with a dead phone battery, I realised I couldn't find a clock on the walls. Somehow all these aspects combined to create a story.

The box is based on a very clear memory I have of being out with friends and digging in the 'forest' next to where the Caithness Glass Factory used to be. We found a box randomly buried, which to our young minds was pretty exciting. It was locked, so we broke it open with a rock.

It contained absolutely nothing.

However, the grassy area around those trees may contain a full archaeological site's worth of Caithness glass from about a three year period of its history. Which may or may not have been acquired from the 'broken and misshapen' crates outside the Caithness Glass Factory – liberated by a small band of young rogues.

My memory is really fuzzy on this bit – officer – so I can neither confirm nor deny that if you were in the market for a wonky giraffe or a grotesquely deformed paperweight, then digging around this area may reveal some secret stashes.

Equal To and Greater Than

My friends with children on the spectrum – and other disabilities – are some of the strongest, most patient and kindest people I know. I will always go out of my way to support them with whatever they need – because they don't like to ask for help. Yet they are generously warm, loving and caring for others. They deserve the best for themselves too.

The children are also amazing. Each of them have their own unique strengths, and it was this that inspired me to write a strong autistic protagonist. We are all born with different strengths. The message of the story is that we should celebrate them and work together to bring the best out of each other.

I was fortunate enough to meet and meditate with the Dalai Lama when he visited the UK in 2008. I was in the third year of my honours degree in psychology. My professor, a top researcher in the field of consciousness and transpersonal psychology, was given a ticket to meet him. Unfortunately, a couple of days before the event something came up and he couldn't go.

So rather than let the ticket go to waste, he gave it to me. Next thing I know I'm in a hall in Nottingham meditating with the man himself, who was also imparting his wisdom to these top academics and spiritual leaders… and me!

The Dalai Lama is credited with one of my favourite quotes which inspires how I try to live my life – 'Be kind whenever possible. It is always possible.' This is represented by Darren in the story – and should be reflected by all of us in society.

Of course, it wouldn't be a story about my childhood in the Highlands if it didn't also contain some element of skipping school.

Background: The old Wick High School had a slight flaw in their system, which we used to our advantage. There would be a 'day sheet' that would be given to each teacher after the morning break.

If you weren't there for register in the morning, you were marked as absent on the day sheet. This let the teachers know that you weren't in school that day, so they wouldn't look for you in class.

However, if you then turn up to school after the day sheet has been distributed, you could get a 'late pass'. This means that you don't need any further signed letters or anything from home to explain your absence, as you are marked on the school system as simply being late for that day.

So the teachers aren't expecting you in class, and the office isn't expecting an explanation. Perfect! Now you can go and do whatever you like with the rest of your day!

Get caught? That's fine because you've already changed your home address to your friend's house, whose parents don't care what letters come through the door – but you can still pick up any exam results posted to you – and just say they were delivered to the school.

And that pesky home phone number? Well, good luck getting somebody to answer the ringing phone at a random phonebox at the top of the forest near the industrial estate.

A foolproof plan, one might say. And it worked well for just over two months. There were about 14 of us at the start. Everybody slowly got caught until there were only 3 of us left. We were eventually discovered that fateful day – sipping shandies in a pub-that-shall-not-be-named, who kindly used to let us keep our pool cues behind the bar.

Still to this day I have no idea how the admin detectives at the school managed to contact our parents – though about 60 late passes in a row was pretty damning evidence. When he brought them out in front of me it was like the end of Crystal Maze, where the contestants are clutching a bunch of golden tickets gathered from The Crystal Dome. My prize was – instead of being instantly expelled, like my two comrades – I was allowed to sit my exams. I was also awarded the bonus prize of being grounded for the rest of my life – technically that's not actually expired, so let's not remind anyone.

Still, the high school has provided great memories for future story characters. One day I was sitting in physics class, wondering where everybody was from my group of rogues, when the admin lady entered the class and told me to pack up my stuff. So I walked with her to the office, convinced I was about to be expelled. But apparently my Uncle Bob had called and my family had to get the train to Inverness that afternoon – so I was to meet them at the station.

Nodding my head solemnly, I looked concerned, told her I understood and then left the school grounds – knowing damn well that I didn't have an Uncle Bob. My suspicions were confirmed when I reached the train station and there – emerging from a phonebox – was an absolute legend who had just gotten me three days off school!

Now, this particular friend had left a window open in his house, on the off-chance that we needed somewhere to hang out during the day. Unfortunately, it wasn't a ground floor window. So when we reached his house, I had to climb on the back wall, hop across to the flat kitchen roof, and then climb in his window. Simple right?

What he had neglected to tell me was that he had a housekeeper. Who just so happened to be at home at the point I entered the house. In fact, she was coming up the stairs as I was coming down it.

I don't know who shit themselves the most.

I eventually managed to explain that my friend had forgotten his key and was waiting at the back door to be let in. The housekeeper then finished her work and left.

After that, we had just made scrambled eggs and were watching The Offspring's *Pretty Fly (For a White Guy)* on a music channel, when we heard a car pull up outside his house.

His mother had come home early.

Shitting myself for the second time in an hour, we legged

it out the back door and hid in his garage, taking the scrambled eggs with us. His mother must have walked into the house and thought the housekeeper had made herself a tasty protein snack on the way out.

I don't know if he ever confessed this to his mother, but I'll make sure she receives a copy of this book.

Back to the story: So while waiting one day for the day sheet to reach the classrooms, a couple of us decided that hiding in the toilets was safer than roaming the streets, because a particularly observant and angry teacher may have been on to us.

For some reason a pen had burst ink all over my hands, no doubt from forging a letter from home for somebody – something I became so proficient in that I knew everybody's parents on a first-name basis.

So I was washing my hands when the previously mentioned angry teacher burst through the door and asked us (loudly) what we were doing out of class. I said I had been sent out to wash my hands, showing him the ink. He accepted this story.

My friend had just quickly thrown his cigarette down the toilet, but the smoke betrayed him. And he was not so fortunate in having a ready-made alibi, so he was marched out of there – and to this day I often wonder what happened to him. They say his screams still haunt the maths block – forever seeking the Embassy Number 1 he never got to finish.

Long story short – I visualised the main character washing his hands in those same toilets while he was out of class.

As for the maths challenge, his nerves around that were based on a memory of the one and only time I put myself forwards for the poetry reading competition in primary school. I don't remember what the poem was – I only remember being whisked away from school, to read something I had only half memorised, to a room full of strangers. Traumatic.

The positive message from all of this is that I dropped out of school at 16, only sitting 1 exam. But now I have a 1st Class Honours Degree and a PhD and endless other qualifications. Not everybody follows the same path in life, and you can change your story at any moment.

The Gala Queen

Two things I used to love as a kid were Halloween and the Wick Gala. Being young, foolish (and tipsy when we shouldn't be) we would dare each other to go to the lane at the bottom end of Green Road Park and show our asses to the cars in the dark.

Their headlights would reveal the full moon as they climbed up Church Street and swung round the corner onto Louisburgh Street. Again, the things we did to entertain ourselves before the internet. Now everybody has their asses out on social media instead!

As an adult who drives – I reflected that maybe it could have gone a bit wrong if we had startled the driver too much. So that's where the idea for this story came from.

My daughter recently spent her first Halloween in Scotland. I took her out guising and she got quite a shock when she realised that, unlike where she was living before, she actually had to tell jokes and earn her treats. It was even funnier when I got home and handed her a knife and a neep – she did well though, finally had it carved out by Christmas… she also writes with her left hand now.

Obviously, the procession that the main character ends up in – the horrific one – is completely made up. The initial gala he attends – the exciting one raising money for charity – is loosely based on my memories of Wick Gala. It's an annual, week-long programme of events, run by amazing volunteers, who raise funds for the town. It brings the community together and is definitely worth a visit.

Revenge of the Green Man

This story was a personal test as an author. I wanted to write something funny, but I have quite a dark and dry sense of humour. So this was my first attempt at writing a dark comedy.

It's tragic in a humorous, but ultimately harmless, kind of way. It reflects the personality and choices that a couple of my friends may make when faced with a similar situation.

I love the music of the '90s and, like most of the UK, I owned the *What's the Story Morning Glory* album, along with numerous other Britpop albums.

The crowning moment of inspiration for this story though came from when I was much younger, playing with friends in Green Road Park. There was a small wall near the roundabout, with a bungalow behind it that was due for demolishing to build newer, nicer bungalows.

Somebody had broken a window into the old bungalow and it contained random items, including a wardrobe that we would dare each other to go in.

One day, one of my friends decided to have a short break from spinning around on the end of a railway sleeper we had wedged into the roundabout. The reason: he needed a poo. Now living quite a few streets away, the much younger me imagined he was going to be gone a while. But he had other ideas.

It was at this point in my young life that I realised that

socially-constructed rules really are just guidelines. It was Bear Grylls, before his time. If you want to leap a garden wall and have a shite in somebody's overgrown garden, you can.

And that's exactly what he did while calling back over the wall for the rest of us to find him some more dock leaves.

Moving on, there was a group of rascals who would dare each other to kick the lamppost of a supposed local 'axeman' until the light went out. Observing this behaviour, it never actually made any sense to me, either from the plausibility of an actual axe-wielding murderer just sitting around his living room waiting for some kids to make his garden a little bit darker, or from a not-wanting-to-be-hacked-to-death-today perspective, if the rumours were true.

At no point during any of these escapades did I ever hear of an axeman appearing, but nevertheless they continued to harass multiple lampposts around the town. Right up until the point of where they tried it outside the police houses, resulting in a hasty jog up Wick riverside in the dark.

So, for some, kicking lampposts out was merely a hobby that kept them fit. Putting windows through and setting bins on fire, though, almost seemed to be the main events in an alternative Olympic Games.

I could imagine even Usain Bolt shaving a few extra seconds off if he was being shot at with a BB gun. The boxing will go ahead as normal – but the venue has been changed to the Bignold Park during lunchtime. A bygone era of entertainment before phones, the internet and maturity as a society took over.

I know Dunnett Forest very well, having stopped by and walked through it many times on my road trips back north. As for some of the other references in this story, well, I guess you may have had to be there at the time. Regarding the dialogue - see the Author's Notes at the end for the absolute headache the accent spellings caused me!

I chose the Green Man after a night drinking at a whisky bar in Stirling. I had brought my Maori friend Tama along on a one-way road trip to Scotland, as I had told him how great Edinburgh was, so he decided to look for bar work there while touring the UK.

I had met up with a couple of other high school friends in our usual bar. One of the handmade pieces of art on the wall was a wooden carving of the face of the Green Man.

Fast forward a few days: I had continued my journey north to Wick with my other road trip buddy Mily – Queen of the Rogues. Tama had secured work and accommodation in Edinburgh and sent us a picture of what he had decided to spend his savings on – a huge forearm tattoo of the Green Man – something to remember his time in Scotland.

The House on Lovers' Lane

Before our nightly shenanigans could begin, our group of friends would usually meet at one end of town. This would be in the middle of a large squared street, if we were on one side of the river. Or on a particular road if we were on the other side.

At the end of this road, there are some big houses with large gardens. The road itself connects to a narrow Lover's Lane which leads down to the riverside.

Being young, foolish and tipsy… (yes, most my younger-self stories start like this – my adult ones just start with the foolish and tipsy part) we would attempt to see who could cut across a particular garden the furthest, without setting off their security light. The dark house always appeared to be abandoned. The rest of the story grew from there.

A stream ran the full length of the field at the end of that road and we would see who could jump the widest gap. That often did not end well.

I always loved the story of Tam o' Shanter. I think I first heard about it while doing Burn's night stuff in primary school. The visual aspects of the story, and the lucky escape, always stuck with me.

Now living in Ayrshire, I thought I would include a nod to this at the start of the story. I have spent many nights throwing sugar on fires and telling ghost stories with friends – possibly influenced by the Midnight Society from *Are You Afraid of the Dark?*

Call of the Nuckelavee

This story is inspired by both Dunnet Beach and Reiss Beach, as well as trips to Orkney. On our first road trip to visit Dunnett Forest and the beach, we parked up far too soon. This meant we tried to traverse the larger sand dunes, via coarse grass and boggy ground. In trainers. It didn't go well but inspired part of this story.

A lot of my memories are of me just running into the sea. If you search YouTube for a video called 'Memories of Scotland - Caithness - Wick, John O'Groats, Dunnet, Reiss & more - 1994/95' then you will see a short video of a younger me running along the beach.

It also contains old home video footage of places around Caithness during 1994 and 1995. It includes the Grey Cairns of Camster and the Kyleburn sweet factory.

Since moving back to Scotland, my daughter is getting used to the sea. We like to wade in when it's a bit choppy and she has experienced the power of it sweeping her legs away. I wanted to capture some of that raw power.

She also wanted to go rockpooling at a ridiculous time of the evening – until I took her down and showed her the vast darkness of the sea at night.

Legendary creatures of Scottish myths have always fascinated me. And judging by the giant kelpie sculptures, a unicorn as a national animal, and a certain elusive monster swimming about Loch Ness – I think I'm in good company.

I was inspired by a legend much closer to home in the Highlands, the kelpie grave within the grounds of St Trothan's Church in Castletown.

Legend has it that a local fisherman found a baby girl wrapped in sealskin on the beach. He took her home and he and his wife raised her as their own. However, even as a child, she had magical powers. This got her banned from the church because she claimed to have seen the devil in the rafters.

She later died in childbirth and was buried at St Trothan's. Her grave has a small hollow which apparently never dries out. Legend says if you stick your foot gently into the hollow and make a wish, it will come true.

Wanting to see her deceased father one more time and her search for answers was inspired by both my own and my close friend's experiences. A lot of us have lost our fathers, myself included. His ashes were scattered to the sea.

I enjoy taking my dog a walk along the beach, as it brings a sense of peace and fires the imagination for my stories. I then wondered what if something happened that at first appeared to be a supernatural symbol of hope, but was actually there to shatter the tranquillity of my beach walk.

Black Dog in the Devil's Bothy

The stresses of modern life have meant that many people suffer from anxiety and depression, or both. In all its forms and degrees of severity, these can be debilitating mental health conditions. And many people go undiagnosed, not seeking the help they need.

This is the story of a woman who lives with the 'black dog' of depression during the day and is tormented by anxious fears at night. It's affected many areas of her life, including work, family and friendships.

In addition to seeking professional help, she has decided to take a break from her normal life. She is attempting natural healing in the form of exercise, sunshine and surrounding herself with natural beauty, of which there is an abundance in the Highlands.

The heat of the pressures of life forces her to lay herself bare to the world.

With this story, I wanted to highlight not only the effect of these mental health conditions but also the ability we have to fight them and heal ourselves. To remind people that there is always more than one choice. That we are only ever a single thought away from opening the door to a different mindset.

I love being surrounded by nature. When I'm not on the beach, I'm usually off on a forest walk. Military training gave me a love for an active lifestyle – always staying fighting fit – which is also positive for my mental health.

Most importantly, I wanted the story to be a message of hope for anybody that finds themselves in a dark place. No matter how lost you feel, the storm will pass.

Diabhal translates to *Devil*. And when the devil appears in stories, it's usually in the form a test between good and evil. In this case, both a literal and metaphorical battle between light and dark.

To quote a rather well-known author:

"Happiness can be found, even in the darkest of times, if one only remembers to turn on the light."
- J.K. Rowling, Harry Potter and the Prisoner of Azkaban

Or in this case, kick a great big hole in a burning wall whilst in your underwear. But the sentiment remains the same. Do whatever it takes to find your light.

On a separate note, I love stories with riddles in them! I have always wanted to write one, so I can now tick that off my author checklist.

Last Train South

The premise of this story is that people need to learn to be kinder to each other.

I have supported friends through some really tough times in their lives. I have seen what they have been through – their anger, tears and raw emotion.

The five stages of grief are denial, anger, bargaining, depression and acceptance. However, with the stresses and anxieties of modern life – it's my personal opinion that very few people reach acceptance – many feel hopelessly stranded at varying levels of depression.

Or if they do reach acceptance with one issue, then life decides to pile up multiple issues – causing you to not only go through these stages for each individual issue but also having to deal with the weight of them all as a whole.

Life's tough. It can often seem like its one thing after another. But the main thing that gets us through hard times? Our support network. Our friends.

I took this idea literally, with a group of friends coming together to help a woman deal with her emotional – and literal – baggage. It's the story of a woman pushed too far. It's vengeful – emotional pain creating physical pain. She reaches acceptance by evening the score.

As an author, it was an exploration of the dark side of love. The what-comes-after.

This all takes place on a train journey that I have taken more than any other – the Wick to Inverness train. Which in real-life is one of the most scenic train routes in the UK. At certain points, you are convinced the train is actually passing through the edge of the sea.

As a human – it doesn't matter whether we are close friends, only acquaintances, or complete strangers. If you need support – reach out to me. If I can help, I will. Be kind whenever possible. It is always possible. A wise man taught me that.

I often think about the story of the boy helping the starfish. I'll give my version of it here, adapted from *The Star Thrower* by Loren Eiseley:

There was an old man who walked along the same beach every morning. Early one morning, he was walking along the shore after a big storm had passed and found the entire beach littered with starfish as far as the eye could see, stretching in both directions.

Off in the distance, he noticed a small boy walking along the beach. The boy kept bending down to pick up an object and throw it into the ocean. The man walked towards the boy and called out "May I ask what you are doing?"

"Throwing starfish into the ocean. The tide has washed them up onto the beach and they can't return to the sea by themselves," the boy replied. "When the sun gets high, they will die, unless I throw them back into the water."

"But there must be tens of thousands of starfish on this beach," said the old man. "I'm afraid you won't be able to make much of a difference."

The boy bent down, picked up another starfish and threw it as far as he could into the ocean. Then he turned to the old man and said: "It made a difference to that one!"

The reason I have included this story is that it represents the way I think. I know there are a lot of problems in the world. I know that every single person has an issue that I might be able to help them with.

Unfortunately, I also know there isn't enough time or resources for me to support and heal them all.

However, that doesn't mean I do nothing. I do everything I can, when I can. Because even if there were tens of thousands of people needing help, you only need to make a difference to one person. That one friend who needs you – go check up on them.

Note: Throwing your friend in the ocean is optional.

Of course, in an ideal world, we would all be helping each other. A beach full of star throwers, making a difference.

Sometimes I barely know the people I help, particularly through my charity work. I just happen to have the answer to what they need. It might be the only interaction that I ever have with them in my life – so I make sure it's a positive one.

We never really know the true impact we have on the people we meet. So my advice would also be to reach out to people. Friends, family, acquaintances, strangers – anybody you can see who is struggling. And yes, even people you haven't always got along with, as they are often going through the toughest times of all. We're all too old now, and not all of us made it. Make peace and the world will remember you more kindly.

So if any of you ever message me saying 'I'm on the train, meet me at Beauly station' – I'll know you're going through something and need my help.

Special thanks to Jodie, who – when asked what this original love story was missing – replied with murder. She says that for all my stories though. Some people are beyond even my help!

Stolen Peace

Fittingly, the final story in the book was the last one I wrote. I wanted to attempt to create a story in a stricter word count, closer to flash fiction length. It was the one story influenced more by my current life, rather than memories.

I enjoy reading and writing in wild places. I liked the idea that a scientific Dr had simply had enough of his academic work and had taken off to spend the rest of his days relaxing, surrounded by nature. What kind of Dr would do such a thing…

I wrote almost all of this book during the COVID-19 lockdown in March and April 2020. A *Marvel* movie marathon was taking place in the same room I was writing in. Therefore, Dr Bruce Banner may also have influenced the story, with its body-empowering serum.

AUTHOR'S NOTES

In the preface, I promised a bit more of my personal story and a conversation about writing dialogue in the Highland accent. Both topics were originally published on my blog, but here are the updated versions:

I grew up in Wick, in Caithness, near John O' Groats in the far north of Scotland. Wick and the surrounding areas have an interesting heritage – from the iron ages to the Norse pagan period. It's believed Wick was originally named from the Norse word *vik*, meaning bay. A Viking town then with an enormous sense of history, adventure, mystery and wonder in its beaches, forests and ruins. Endless inspiration for stories and characters.

It's a small town filled with decent, good-hearted, funny and hard-working people, my family included. The majority of my family are Scottish. My dad had also spent part of his childhood growing up in Wick and we had attended the same secondary school, Wick High School.

My grandparents ran a tearoom in Strathpeffer and over the years the rest of us became spread out across the Highlands. The A9 north from Inverness is basically the trunk of my family tree, with each of us settled on the branches along the way (minus the few who smuggled themselves south of the border).

Wick has grown over the years that I have been away. What I remember as fields is now a retail park. The Caithness Glass factory that fascinated me as a child is closed down long ago. The 'forest' next to it that my friends and I used to play in as children is now mostly fenced off.

I have been back up nearly every single year since I left, sometimes two or three times, on 1,500 mile road trips. Sadly, in the name of progress, my primary school has been knocked down (North Primary School) and my high school has been replaced, a modern one built behind it.

Lots of new things that the town needed have sprung up over the years though, providing job opportunities and a great quality of life for the community.

We, the people, have changed too. Our friends that we have seen laying half-dead in fields, drunkenly rambling about the moon, are now middle-managers and have heavy machinery licenses. Fiery personalities have turned their attention away from fighting each other, to fighting for a better community and world for all of us. Feuds matured into friendships, because at the end of the day, we are all in this together, a part of each other's history and life stories.

Many of us became parents, a generation of mini versions of ourselves filling the gaps we vacated. And in turn, we took jobs and roles in the places our parents and grandparents previously filled. Students became teachers and the great cycle of life continued.

This came home to me when I visited my old primary school, just before it was knocked down. One of my primary teachers showed me around my old P7 classroom and it brought back so many memories. And she worked there with somebody from the same year as me in high school. The cycle of life.

Every generation knows tragedy, and ours was no different. We have lost a lot of good friends and family along the way. The lives of beautiful, talented and amazing people cut way too short. Which is why those of us who are left should spend our time wisely, supporting each other and the future generations, doing as much good in the world as we can.

This is one of the main reasons that I decided to drop out of the academic rat race and the high-flying international business world I had built, in order to dedicate myself to charity work. My PhD, Dr title, academic awards, business success, publications, military medal and everything else I accumulated don't mean anything compared to having the ability to help somebody who needs it.

I'll only get involved with an academic or community project now if it's doing some good in the world. I support equality and enjoy writing strong male and female protagonists, of all cultures and ethnicities. Characters who are strong because of their disabilities, and characters who find hope and strength beyond their anxiety, depression and trials of everyday life.

I write about people going through extraordinary things, but with a message that can translate to the real world. It's okay if things aren't positive all the time. It's normal to feel scared, sad, angry or annoyed with events that are happening around you, and to you. This is the human experience. And there is always hope for something better in the next chapter.

The trouble with being away from where I grew up for so long is that there are people I care about deeply, that I haven't seen in many years. As my generation slowly marches towards middle-age, I have decided I need to rectify that.

So there are a few more proper catch-ups to do. I want to dedicate the time to really get to know people again, instead of just randomly dropping a message out of the blue, helping resolve an issue, then disappearing again for years at a time!

The memories and friendships I have from my childhood are still strong, and now I'm living back in Scotland my road trips will be more frequent. I can still visit the beaches I played on as a child. Reiss Beach, in particular, is one of the most beautiful beaches I have ever been to. And you could still find me having a dip in the North Sea (even the Trinkie) as late as October and November.

Moving on to the second thing I promised to discuss: accents, both my own and my characters.

The beautiful lilt of a Scottish accent. It's a wonderful thing to hear, but as I discovered, an absolute headache to spell each word so it sounds just right to the ear.

You would think writing dialogue for Scottish characters would be an easy thing for me to do, seeing as it's my default childhood accent. But apparently being a Highlander comes with some distinct quirks, pronunciations and words that seemingly aren't used outside of the very north of Caithness.

So while writing dialogue for *Revenge of the Green Man* I was faced with having to spell every word with the authenticity that I used to pronounce it with growing up. After living for 21 years down in England though, my own accent has changed to something unique.

I followed the family tradition of spending our childhood in the north of Scotland, before moving away and joining the military. Like me, my father moved away from Scotland and joined the military (he joined the Army – I joined the RAF like my uncle).

Eventually, we all make our way back to Scotland, but not before going off to explore the world. And those family members who never left make fun of our changed accents.

When I first moved down, nobody could understand me. Coming from Wick, I had a broad Highland accent and a vocabulary that you won't find in any dictionary. One example: I would say "D'ye ken…" (as in, do you know) and everybody thought I was saying "Chicken".

Even my own family on my mother's side had to listen really carefully, and I found myself deliberately putting on an English accent in order to be understood. It was frustrating for me, having just turned 16, to not be listened to (or thought of as the guy that went around saying "chicken" all day). And even though I was proud of my Scottish accent, I knew I had to work on overcoming what had now become a barrier for me.

Over time this deliberate changing of my accent became my norm, a mixture of both Scottish and English. This was further chipped away when I joined the military. Exposed to accents from all over the UK, we all began to speak like each other, stealing words and inflections here and there.

And I didn't just live in one part of England, I travelled about, a bit of time in the West Midlands, East Midlands, South Coast, Northampton, Coventry and then a final five years in The Cotswolds, with their gentrified Oxfordshire Queen's English-esque newsreader accents (or so it sounded like to me).

This was in addition to time spent abroad, travelling around Europe, a month in Norway here, a month in Belgium there, a total of eight months in Northern Ireland. Then living with a variety of UK and international students at two different universities – I can now mimic any accent in the world!

My English friends could still hear the Scottish accent, especially after a whisky or two. But my Scottish friends could mostly hear the English accent.

Moving back to Scotland, to Ayrshire, my Scottish accent has started to come back. And I can finally be understood again, no matter which accent slips out my mouth – though I still get funny looks when it switches mid-sentence, or my brain attempts to speak both pronunciations at once!

So I had a conversation with friends and family who had just proofread the first draft of *Revenge of the Green Man*. I had attempted to balance readability, while still allowing the characters to speak their native Scots language.

And I had failed.

Reading it aloud, it was obvious that the spellings looked correct, but didn't sound quite right to the ear when spoken out loud.

This is where the can of worms was opened.

Now living within the West Central Scots accent area, it had influenced the way I wrote. I hear the Ayrshire and Lanarkshire words (awa, braw, wean), mixed with Glaswegian influences, as we are so close to the city.

So here's an example of what I was facing:

The word '*what*'. I had decided to used '*whit*'. However, this didn't sound right in certain circumstances. This is where we realised the singular '*what*' and the plural '*what's*' became different spellings entirely, with the plural becoming an Aberdonian-esque '*fit's*'.

So the general rule is, for the North East of Scotland, drop the *Wh* and replace it with an *F*. However, even that rule was broken from time to time. And changed yet again depending on where the word came in the sentence, with '*Fit's*' at the start and '*Whit*' at the end.

Plural: What's that about = Fit's 'at aboot
Singular: My car, that's what! = Ma car, thas whit!
Rulebreaker: What are you on about = Fit ye on aboot

This is the best my proofreaders and I could come up with. Even the word *that* was spelt differently in two of those sentences. The basic premise of my North East Scotland accent is to say as many words as you can, as quickly as possible. This means dropping most the letters in a sentence and stringing the words together!

As my friend pointed out: "Am joos realizin' it's pritty hard til capture eh auld week axeint."

And he wisny wrong. Cos we dinny joos add n' '*ae*' on eh end o' stuff n' be done wi' it.

Adding an '*ae*' onto the end of words seems like a simple fix. But we quickly realised that, while the '*ae*' works well for some words like dinnae, it doesn't work for gonnae, because we actually pronounce it gunna.

But then the '*ae*' also gives it a more Glaswegian/Central

Belt sound. Like the TV show Chewing the Fat: Am gonnae no dae that. But the Highland lilt lifts more at the end of certain words. So to recreate the quicker lift, we went with dinny. And 'disny bother me' works for us. And can't becomes canny, rather than cannae.

And then there are the random words I have used my whole life. I have never in my life called a *seagull* a seagull or gull. It's a scorrie. Even Wick Academy Football Club are nicknamed The Scorries. But everywhere I have ever been, even over here in the west of Scotland, they haven't got a clue what I am on about if a wis til say a scorrie scoot on ma heed.

So basically, we decided to create and agree on the spelling of our own dialect. This is the freedom that writers have when writing dialogue. These are my characters, this is how they speak. As long as it is believable and consistent.

There'll no doubt be people who still think we haven't got it quite right, but then there are words that even people who live in the same town pronounce differently. And the reason for that? Dialect changes over time.

The words my grandparents used weren't the same words my parents used, which again were changed slightly by my own generation. So dialect words and pronunciations become generation-based.

An example of this is my grandparents used to say '*laskie*' and '*boygie*' when referring to girls and boys respectively. However, the generation above me would say '*lassie*' and '*chiel*'. Then my own generation kept '*lassie*', but it seemed

133

more common to say '*loon*' or '*guy*' for a male. And that's just the changing influences within my own family.

Every generation of kids always seems to make up their own words and phrases that define their era. So you end up with a mix of dialects and words, with people in the same town, at the same school, even living in the same house, having different individual influences.

A can of worms.

So when you get handed a dictionary or guide to Scottish dialects, you have to pay attention to the age of the writer and how it has influenced their interpretations. Want to write a book set in the distant past of the highlands? You'll be using different spellings and words than if you wrote a contemporary story of modern-day highland life.

So what I have also learned is that, if you want to have an authentic-sounding Scottish dialect for your characters, then where possible you need to ask people from that specific area, and the correct age group.

Don't ask a Scottish person from any other dialect region. My family and friends from across the country started sharpening their claymores to tear apart my dialogue because they all swore they had the one true Scots to rule them all – '*there can be only one!*'

When the dust settled, we attempted to make a glossary to use solely for my collection of stories, consistent within their specific time period, as authentically true as we could achieve.

Here's some o' whit a bunch o' weekers came up wi':

What = Fit/Whit (depending on context)
What's = Fit's
Have = Hev
Haven't = Hevny
The = Eh (or drop a letter or two: e.g. th'night, t'get)
Maybe = Mibbe
No = Nae/Naw (depending on sentence)
Not = No'
Do = Dae (or D'ye for 'do you')
To = Til (99% of the time, an occasional tae depending on context)
My = Ma
I'm = Am
Out = Oot
About = Aboot
With = Wi'
Sold = Selt
Told = Telt
Yes = Aye
House = Hoose
You = Ye (You'se for when referring to more than one person)
Know = Ken
Of = O'
Our = Oor
Your = Yer
You're = Ye're
For = Fur
Like = Lek
Make = Mek
Round = Roond

Going to = Gunna
Can't = Canny
Won't = Willny
Doesn't = Disny
Didn't = Didny
Give = Gi'
Down = Doon
Town = Toon
This = 'is
Hundred = Hunner (won a close vote over hunnert)
Now = Noo
Too = n'all

It wasn't perfect but covered enough bases for me to write consistent and believable dialogue. Throw in a few swear words and my characters were complete. Irvine Welsh, I felt your pain of trying to spell the raw Scots dialect in a true manner. Who would have thought it would be so difficult to write in my natural accent?

So that's it.

If you enjoyed reading this book, please leave a review so others can discover me and my writing. It supports us authors and inspires us to write!

Head over to my website to become a follower of my blog. This will let you see when I publish a new blog post, usually once a month. It sometimes includes free stories.

Until next time, be kind to each other.

Aaron Mullins

ABOUT THE AUTHOR

Aaron Mullins

Dr Aaron Mullins is an award-winning, internationally published psychologist. He started Birdtree Books Publishing where he worked as Editor-in-Chief. He partnered with World Reader Charity and sponsored English lessons in an under-tree school in India, before moving on to new ventures.

Aaron's work for the National Centre for Entrepreneurship in Education stimulated business growth throughout Saudi Arabia, Malaysia, India and Nigeria, as well as enhancing entrepreneurial research within the UK.

Aaron taught academic writing at Coventry University. As a fiction author, he's known for exploring the darker side of psychology in his work. He creates business guides for entrepreneurs, writing guides for fellow authors, and is also the designer behind the Mullins Made clothing brand.

Now semi-retired from academia and moved back to Scotland, he devotes most of his time to charity work, travelling and writing on the beach.

www.aaronmullins.com

BOOK PREVIEW: OUT NOW

Mullins Collection of Best New Fiction

Explore worlds populated with strange creatures. Ghouls that feed in the darkness of the London underground in *The Orphaned City* and the strange patient who stalks the halls of a mental asylum in *Inferiority Complex*. Discover worlds where humans are the most curious of all, the charming smile of the mysterious Jack in *Knowing Jack* and the devious mind of Red in *The Path I Set Upon*.

Will the next story spark into life a new idea, the kind that Jake develops from an overheard conversation in *Dreamworld*. Or question our very existence, like the revelations of Professor Westerham in *Reflection*. It might even lead to a dangerous hunt for untold riches, which Ryan experiences in *The Hassam Legacy*.

You may discover a love for stories you wouldn't have considered before. Fiction does that to you. It draws you into its welcoming embrace. Sometimes the welcome is warm, like the strength of Helen after dealing with death in *Coming of Age*. Other times you feel an icy chill as the story grips you, like the terror that claws at Meg when she hears her parrot speak in *Scared to Death*.

Nine different worlds are waiting to be explored. Each hides a secret, a twist that awaits discovery by an adventurous reader. Welcome to our worlds.

First published 2012.

www.aaronmullins.com

BOOK PREVIEW: OUT NOW

Mullins Collection of Best New Horror

Horror.

The stories that keep you awake at night. The tales that have you checking underneath the bed... or wondering whether that really is just a shadow in the corner.

In this collection, you will find early stories from four horror writers, all guaranteed to instil a feeling of dread deep within your bones as your shaking fingers struggle to turn the page.

A dark secret is revealed in *My Natalie*, a tale of vengeful love. A home with a hidden past threatens to destroy a young family in *The House*.

The restless spirit of a young girl has to deliver an important message in *Phantom Memory*. Finally, thrill-seeking Melanie gets more than she bargained for as she explores the mysterious festival in *The Secrets of Hidden Places*.

The horror awaits…

First published 2013.
www.aaronmullins.com

Printed in Great Britain
by Amazon